# The invitation was every man's dream...

"I'd like to have my way with you...." Willa brushed her fingertips over Joel's skin. "But first..."

*No. No firsts.* "First?"

"Will you tell me what you want me to do?"

At that moment, Joel couldn't remember ever wanting a woman with this degree of possessive fierceness. It bothered him, but it didn't keep him from saying, "What I want you to do is simple. Let me make love to you."

Willa stared at him over her shoulder, her mouth a spoiled pout. "That defeats the purpose of the question, doesn't it?"

"Darlin', right now I don't give a damn about the question. Only about the answer."

She tilted her head back and her bound ponytail brushed his bare chest. It was torture.

He hissed out a low breath. "If I don't touch you soon, I'm afraid I'm gonna explode."

When she turned in his arms he saw that she'd caught her lower lip between her teeth to hold back a grin. "Are you saying," she asked innocently, "we may be dealing with an accidental shooting, Detective Wolfsley?"

Dear Reader,

Well, it's been a while since my last Temptation novel appeared. What have I been doing when I should have been writing, you ask? Well, getting married, for one thing! A Temptation author can never do too much research into the process of falling in love. Am I right?

This month I'm pleased to offer you *The Badge and the Baby,* my contribution to Temptation's exciting new BACHELORS & BABIES miniseries. And in October, look for *Four Men & a Lady,* a high school 15th-reunion story that also celebrates Temptation's 15th anniversary. You think *The Big Chill* was fun? Wait till you meet Ben and Heidi and Quentin and Randy and Jack. Which guy gets the girl? Ah, that's between me and Heidi. For now.

Happy reading!

Alison Kent

## Books by Alison Kent

### HARLEQUIN TEMPTATION
594—CALL ME
623—THE HEARTBREAK KID
664—THE GRINCH MAKES GOOD

# Alison Kent
# THE BADGE AND THE BABY

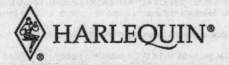

## HARLEQUIN®

TORONTO • NEW YORK • LONDON
AMSTERDAM • PARIS • SYDNEY • HAMBURG
STOCKHOLM • ATHENS • TOKYO • MILAN • MADRID
PRAGUE • WARSAW • BUDAPEST • AUCKLAND

Thanks to Transworld's ninth-floor crew for being such good sports. Enjoy your cameos. Thanks to the women of Genie—Khrys and Barbara especially—for setting me straight on baby things and broken legs.
Thanks to Bill Corgan and The Smashing Pumpkins for "Adore" and the incredible "Daphne Descends."
Thanks to my own personal stuntman/scene blocker/idea guy/research assistant who also cooks and cleans and has the patience of a saint. I couldn't do any of this without you.

ISBN 0-373-25841-0

THE BADGE AND THE BABY

# 1

JOEL WOLFSLEY had a thing about eyes.

He'd seen 'em scared: gang-tough teenage eyes watching life bleed from their own bodies to the pavement beneath them. He'd seen 'em wild: doped-up junkie eyes, strung out and flying high on a one-way, last-time trip. He'd seen 'em lie: backing up bald-faced, through the teeth, full of "It wasn't me, Officer, I swear you got the wrong guy" stories.

But none of those eyes had the kick of the big baby-blues facing him now. He was a goner. He knew it. Backed into a wall. No partner to cover his rear. Beyond the point where cunning and wits were enough to save his hide. He should've been ready for this. Should've known the time would come when his one admitted weakness would be his undoing.

Because Detective Joel, the Big Bad Wolf, Wolfsley was a sucker for his sisters.

All four of them had used that brotherly weakness to their advantage at one time or another. They'd even sided against him on more than one occasion, representing quadruply unfair four-to-one odds. This time it was sister number one who'd arrived on his front porch. She had both barrels loaded.

The first round squirmed from her mother's arms into her uncle's one-elbow, hooked-around-the-middle hold. The ten-month-old gurgles and giggles and Bambi-brown eyes, were making it hard for Joel to say no.

"I don't know, Jen," he began for the third time before his sister hurried to make up his mind.

"Leigh won't be a bit of trouble, will you, Punkin?" Jennifer Collins tickled her daughter's chubby chin. The baby hung like a potato sack over Joel's shoulder. "You'll be a sweet girl for Uncle Joel this evening, won't you? So Mommy can go see Daddy for a few days?"

Joel watched his distracted sister turn and busy herself checking Leigh's diaper bag, muttering as she ticked off baby wipes and baby powder, diapers and formula. He shared a sideways glance with the baby, rubbing his nose to hers. A stream of drool dribbled from her four-toothed grin to his chest.

"Way to go, Scout," Joel teased, hefting the baby back to his side and frowning down at her impishly innocent face. "And my best T-shirt, too."

Jennifer whirled around and was back at Joel's side before he could blink. "Did she spit up? She just had a bottle. I should've warned you."

"C'mon, Jen. Lighten up." Basket-case hysteria wasn't Jen's style, even when she was doing her best sister-to-big-brother sweet-talkin'. He didn't like seeing her this bent out of shape. "A little spit never hurt a guy."

Heel of her hand pressed to her forehead, Jennifer took a deep breath, blew it out slowly and smiled up at her brother. Then she fired the second round of ammunition. "Sorry, Joel. It's just that I haven't seen Rob in a month. If I miss this chance, I swear I'm going to come unglued."

His sister's marriage to Robert Collins was the exact relationship Joel would wish for had he any intention of marrying. He didn't, which only made him want the best for those fortunate enough to share what Jen and Rob had shared.

"All that's left in the van is the playpen," Jennifer was saying, pushing back a cascade of red-gold curls with one hand, the other resting on her hip as she scanned the room Joel had decorated in a minimalist style of early bachelor. "Let me get that and you'll be all set. Leigh should go down around seven-thirty."

Joel nodded and nipped at Leigh's tiny fingers as she probed behind his lips for his tongue. When he looked up from the baby and back at his sister, he found Jennifer checking her watch as if she had no idea why she was looking.

"Mom and Dad should've been back by now." Distraction left her voice shaken. "I called the lake house yesterday and left a message. No one answered when I tried again this afternoon. They must be on their way home. I left another message on their machine at the house so they'll know you have Leigh. They ought to be here by ten at the latest to pick her up."

Joel watched his sister tick off her list of who, what, when, where and why. The one thing she'd left off mentioning was Leigh's regular sitter. "What about Terri? You couldn't get hold of her? You know I don't mind sitting with Scout here but...criminy, Jen. Don't cry."

Jennifer looked upward and blinked hard. "Dammit, Joel. If my mascara runs I'm going to kill you."

And by the look in her eyes she was exactly that desperate. None of his sisters ever minced words or resorted to the unquestionable power of female tears. If Jen was this close to crying, she'd reached the end of her rope. He wasn't about to be her hangman.

Time to ease the noose he seemed to have inadvertently tightened. He shook his head and lightly chuckled, which caused Leigh to giggle, which brought a watery smile back to Jennifer's face.

"Better." He stroked a finger down his sister's nose. She rewarded him with a more solidly confident smile. Ah, yes. That was his Jennifer. He matched her grin. "Now, go get the playpen before you forget—or I change my mind."

Jennifer stood on tiptoe to give him a hug. "Oh, Joel, you're the best." She stepped back, straightened her bright gold sweater. "You know I wouldn't be here if I wasn't desperate. I didn't even know Rob was coming until he called yesterday from his flight to New York. He'll be in the States a week before it's back to Kuwait."

Jennifer's expression reflected the wistful longing of her sigh. "There hasn't been time to make half the arrangements I need to."

Joel's protective instincts kicked in. "I'll make sure there's a cruiser in the neighborhood to keep an eye on the house. What about the mail and newspapers?"

She nodded. "I did get that taken care of. Howie Jr. is going to pick up both every day, mow the yard tomorrow after school and feed and water Shadow. He was pretty jazzed about the chance to make a few bucks."

No doubt. Joel was familiar with the fifteen-year-old son of his sister's neighbor—more familiar than Jennifer probably realized. Responsibility was a good thing for any teen. A great thing for this one in particular. Now Joel would get the chance to see if Howie had learned his lesson during those sixty hours of community service.

"I'll give Howie a call in a couple of days. Make sure he's really working for that paycheck."

"You mean you're going to put the fear of the Big Bad Wolf into the poor boy." Digging her keys from the black hole of her woven bag, Jennifer shook her head and gave Joel a sisterly critical tsk-tsk. "You can't quit working even for a minute, can you?"

"No, ma'am," Joel answered, hoisting Leigh above his head to the airborne baby's squeals of delight. "Gotta whip these whelps into shape early. Let 'em know who's in charge."

"You're a ruthlessly honorable man, Detective Wolfsley," Jennifer said, faking a terrible Deep South drawl and a swoon. "Why, I feel as safe as a little ol' bug in a rug knowing I'm protected by the likes of your big teeth."

"The better to eat you with, my dear." He growled and blew a quick raspberry on Leigh's tummy, exposed beneath the frilly ruffles of her white dress. Turning a wolf's predatory eye on Jennifer, he lifted a brow. "Playpen. Now. Then get your butt in gear before you miss your flight."

She didn't give him a chance to change his mind.

She raced out the door, returned in less than two minutes with the playpen, managed final instructions and cooing goodbyes to her daughter in the next five, and then she was out the door again.

Thirty seconds later, she'd backed her minivan down the crushed-shell drive and disappeared into the shadows of the tall pines on either side of the long road.

Joel stood in the open doorway and watched Jennifer go. He was really going to have to talk to his sister about that lead foot, he noted, as the cloud of dust raised by her mad dash settled back down on the dirt road. Shaking his head, he went inside, pulled the door closed and turned to Leigh.

"Well, Scout. It's just you and me," he said to the now wriggling baby who had tired of her uncle's charms and was ready to see the world. Or at least what in the world of his house she could get into from a height of two feet.

Joel set her down on her semi-steady feet, cringed when she overcompensated for a wobbly right step with a way too long left, then watched her take off toward the kitchen at the same speed her mother had used to rocket out of his drive minutes ago.

Snagging his cane from where he'd hooked it over the front doorknob, he swung his knee-high walking cast forward and wondered if he'd ever catch the munchkin.

Then he wondered how much grief he could save himself by hanging on to the Big Bad Wolf around his sisters.

THREE HOURS LATER, Joel lay propped in the corner of his navy leather sofa with Leigh fast asleep on his chest.

His parents still weren't home. Calls to friends at the lake as well as to neighbors near their northwest Houston home left Joel as clueless as before he'd picked up the phone.

Sister number two, Carolyn, lived in Chicago with her husband who traded stocks on the floor of the exchange. She hadn't spoken to their parents since a quick call on Good Friday the weekend before.

"You know Mom and Dad," she'd told Joel from her car phone en route from the office of her interior design firm where she'd been working late.

"If they left the lake house early like Jennifer said, that gave them time to go antiquing on the way home. No doubt they ended up halfway to Oklahoma and decided to spend the night. I'm sure they'll be home tomorrow."

Sister number three, Moira, lived in New Mexico where she took leather and beads and shards of glass and made bizarre jewelry that earned her a mint and a name and a permanent display in an exclusive gallery.

"You know Mom and Dad," she'd told Joel when he reached her in her studio. "Any chance to get away for a few days of fishing and they'll take it. Wouldn't surprise me a bit if they're putting all that Christmas camping gear to use. I'm sure they'll be home in a day or two."

His sisters. All so sure. Just like most women, he mused.

Sister number four, Annie, lived in LA where she attended USC's School of Cinema and Television. He hadn't talked to her yet, though he'd left her a message between round one of feeding Leigh bananas and carrots and round two of washing what didn't make it into her mouth down the bathtub drain.

It was bad enough struggling in and out of the tub for his own one-legged showers. Hunkering down to Leigh's level with one leg that didn't want to hunker down had been a pain in the...well, everything.

The muscles in his leg burned like an inferno. He doubted the past four hours of Olympic-caliber endurance athletics were what his doctor considered "taking it easy." No doubt he'd hear about it during his checkup tomorrow morning.

And hear about it ten years from now when Leigh complained that he couldn't slide into home worth a dime with that bum leg. He'd have to remind her then that tonight's marathon caused his leg more damage than the bullet that had torn through the muscles the month before.

The phone rang. He pressed the handset before the chime roused the baby. "Yeah?"

"Nice greeting, Wolf Man. Sounds like I'm going to have to come home and give you an attitude adjustment."

Twenty-year-old bluster. Joel smiled. "Hey, Annie. You got Spielberg beating down your door yet?"

"Check back with me next week. After the film festival," Annie said, a triumphant tone to her voice.

"All right, Li'l Sister. When do I get to see your name scroll by in the credits?"

"If you were here, you could see it Wednesday. But since you're not, you'll have to wait in line with the rest of the commoners." She laughed, oh so full of her cocky young self. "Of course, I'm sure you'll get a full report from Mom and Dad when they get back to town."

Oh, hell. Joel rested his free palm on Leigh's diapered rump and sat forward. Annie had his full attention. "You want to run that one by me again?"

"They called me from the lake house Friday to wish me a happy birthday, which you still have not done, by the way…"

"Aw, Annie." Joel glanced at the addressed and stamped envelope propped on his fireplace mantel. "I didn't forget. I just didn't…remember."

"Hmm. I thought you said you'd been shot in the leg. Not the head."

"Funny girl," Joel said, but his thoughts had already moved from the missed birthday to his missing parents. "Finish telling me about Mom and Dad."

Voices in the background called Annie's name. "In a minute," she yelled directly into the receiver. "Okay. When Dad called, I told him about the film festival. He and Mom decided to come see their youngest in action while they could still get in for free."

Joel stuck his finger to his left ear and wiggled. Annie must yell a damn good "Cut." He moved the receiver to the right ear. "So you're telling me they're on their way to California?"

"Yep. Should be here by Tuesday morning. My show is Wednesday. If they leave after that on

Thursday, that would put them home by Sunday I'm sure."

"Jen thought they'd be home tonight." Jen *promised* him they'd be home tonight. Jen was *sure* they'd be home tonight.

Just like Carolyn was *sure* they'd gone antiquing.

Just like Moira was *sure* they'd gone fishing.

Joel was *sure* he was in big trouble.

"You know Mom and Dad," Annie said, an echo of the others. "They're worse about exercising their prerogative to change their minds than a group of ten women. I have a feeling they were packed and ready to hit the road when I talked to them Friday. They just changed destinations midexit."

Annie paused at the sound of her name being called one more time. This time Joel moved the phone.

"Sorry 'bout that. Anyway, you want me to have them give you a ring when they show?" She barely took a breath before going on. "Is that why you wanted to hear from me, other than to offer me belated birthday wishes, of course?"

It was, but it sure didn't matter now. "Yeah, but don't worry about it. I'll talk to them when they get home."

"Okay, well, I've got to go. Love you, Wolf Man," she said and the line went dead.

Joel pressed the disconnect and set the portable on the hardwood floor. Leigh raised her head, turned to the other cheek and snuggled her fist into her mouth—all without opening her eyes. Her breath came in tiny comforting gusts of warmth against his bare skin.

It was ten o'clock Sunday night. Jen had already

flown out of Bush Intercontinental on her way to JFK. Sisters two, three and four all lived out of state as did Rob's family. And Joel had to make the trek to the doctor in the morning. Leigh's regular sitter was a high-school junior. She had classes in the morning, as did Howie Jr.

And even if Howie were available, there was no way Joel would trust him to take care of this baby. Left in that teen's hands, Jen's dog, Shadow, would be lucky to eat.

Ah, well. This was what family was about. Being there for each other. Joel enjoyed being there in time of need. Had always enjoyed being there. In fact, this was the first time he'd hesitated. If not for being laid up, he'd have said yes before Jen had even explained. But he didn't want to let her down by not being there one hundred percent.

Leigh deserved his best. So did Jen and all the family members gathered under the Wolfsley umbrella. This far-flung group of crazy siblings, in-laws and outlaws allowed him to exercise his fatherly and brotherly urges as well as those of son and uncle. He needed that.

Because he wouldn't have family of his own.

His calling was to serve and protect, a career that put him in danger, at risk. He accepted both, had taken on the responsibility with his eyes wide open.

But he couldn't do his job at the level of competence he required of himself if he had to consider the consequences for loved ones. If he had to second-guess every decision to reach for his weapon. If he was distracted by a memory of a wife or child, when a perp was cornered five feet away.

One or the other, career or family, would suffer. He'd seen it happen to co-workers often enough to prove the myth. And he refused to choose. He loved his sisters, adored every niece and nephew they'd provided him to spoil.

It was enough, this extended family surrounding him. It was enough.

"Well, Scout. It's just you and me," he said, then snuggled back and closed his eyes.

THEY CALLED HIM the Big Bad Wolf.

Willa Grace Darling knew that about him. Knew there were plenty of people afraid of her neighbor. Not your normal law-abiding citizens, of course. No. Those would find him as welcome as the warmth of a fire on a night of chilled bones and breath-frosted air.

But others who couldn't claim a bean of a brain when it came to rights and wrongs feared his wolf-ish bite. As well they should.

Willa took a breath, took a moment to focus, took another to enjoy the view—a purely aesthetic undertaking of course. She smiled, so very glad that she was a woman with an appreciation of things earthy and elemental, and watched him cross the back lawn of her cottage to the kennels where she was feeding the three dogs boarding with her at present.

The Big Bad Wolf was definitely big, though not in a hulkish sort of way. He did work out. The way his T-shirt stretched to accommodate his biceps told that tale. If truth be known, he was probably no more than six foot one or two, though the width through his shoulders and chest topping both flat abs and narrow hips gave the impression of a few extra inches.

Wolfish was a good description. Lean. Wary. Alert. One of a pack who made his way alone. Perhaps not entirely accurate, but Willa liked the capricious notion. Cocking her head to the side, she absently stroked Tic Toc, the pit-bull mix in the first pen. Together they followed Joel's approach.

He always favored black and gray and today was no exception. Black jeans. Gray T-shirt, this one emblazoned with the seal and motto of his employer. It smacked of authority, of pride in a job well done. Funny. All that from a T-shirt.

She was quite aware that clothing had little to do with that undeniable, undefinable *thing* that made this man a man. One she'd never been able to keep her eyes from.

Willa had lived next door to him now for going on a year. He kept an ungodly work schedule, cooking out regularly on the redwood deck he'd built behind his house, pushing himself physically, relentlessly, on marathon-length runs and endless sessions of lifting weights. She'd observed much about him, but had learned little. She had yet to satisfy her unhealthy curiosity about why he never brought a woman home.

Or why, in twelve months, he hadn't made a move in her direction when her harmlessly understated flirtation had spawned an obvious, distinct male interest.

She lowered her lashes and looked away, then lifted them and glanced his direction. He was a man's man. But a woman's man most of all.

His hair was light, a layering of sunbleached

blond and golden brown, though she'd been close enough the times they'd talked to see strands of pure white that put his age past thirty. And those not earned by the years were certainly earned on the job. It couldn't be easy, law enforcement. So much danger. So many risks. She admired him for that, as well.

He got closer and she moved on to the second pen, making kissy-face with the retriever pup named Loverboy who was determined to distract her attention. She gave the dog a ten for effort. But it was hard to distract the distracted. Willa slanted her gaze to the side.

Joel's gait was less fluid than usual, what with the cast he swung forward with each step and the cane he used to balance the rhythm, yet the way he moved was still worth the price of admission.

Big? Yes. Wolf? She could buy it. But she wasn't so sure about "Bad."

Especially with a little girl baby dressed all in white bouncing in the crook of his elbow.

"Willa," he said in greeting, reaching her at last.

"Joel." She lowered her gaze and smiled to herself. From the pail she carried, she scooped out another cup of kibble for Loverboy and emptied the last half cup into the final boarder's tiny bowl. She'd get to the rescued dogs once she'd finished with her paying customers.

And once she found out what brought the Wolf from his lair.

At Willa's single sharp whistle, her own dog, Gordy, padded across the lawn from the shade of the shed where he'd been resting. He held the business end of a water hose in his mouth, the green rubber tubing spooling behind him through the grass.

Destination determinedly in mind, the dog acknowledged the baby's sudden burst of excited babbling with the barest lift of one ear. Willa, however, looked up all the way and met Joel's gaze.

He shifted the little girl's diapered seat, and nailed Willa a look of impressed regard. "That dog's got you spoiled."

Willa took the spray nozzle from Gordy's mouth and rewarded her loyal black-and-white friend with a scratch behind both ears. "Did you know border collies have been trained to carry anything—even a tempting sack lunch—for miles? On no command but a whistle? And deliver it all in one piece?"

"Your own personal pizza delivery."

Amused, she nodded. "Something like that. Though I'm not sure Gordy could deliver a pizza unscathed. He has a thing for pepperoni."

"A dog after my own heart."

Willa looked from the man to the beast who had so captured her affections. "Mine, too." The dog sat at her feet, his eyes on her face, listening, listening. That devotion earned him an extra scratch for good measure.

"So, Detective," she said, nodding toward the infant. "I see you've been busy since last time we spoke."

Joel's smile was that of a man in love. "This doll baby is my niece, Leigh."

Hearing her name, the infant's attention shifted from the dog to Joel. She clapped her hands together and then clapped them on her uncle's face.

"Hey, now, Scout. Uncle abuse will result in a permanent mark on your record."

Doing all she could to keep a straight face, Willa aimed a stream of fresh water at the three bowls she'd just emptied and rinsed. "She definitely has trouble written all over her. Don't you, Leigh?"

Again Leigh responded to her name, this time issued from a stranger's lips. Her white-blond curls and big brown eyes the picture of a Raphaelite angel. She turned to take in Willa's face. Then she saw Tic Toc. And Loverboy. And Mickey, the miniature schnauzer. The baby's deafening squeals set two of the dogs to barking. Willa quieted her canine children while Joel calmed his niece.

Adjusting his weight between cast and cane, Joel nuzzled Leigh's neck until she giggled madly. Then he turned a full male grin Willa's way. "I'm about to need a leash and a harness just so I can keep up with her."

Glancing up through branches overhead, feeling the sough of breeze touching her face, Willa released her breath before looking back at that grin. "Surely that's not why you're here."

"What? A leash and a harness? It's a thought." He tried for a straight face and failed. "Just kidding—" The baby began begging in strident tones to be let down. "What I really need is a muzzle."

Willa only let him get away with the comment because she knew he wasn't serious. Joel wore the label of family man with as much pride as he wore his uniform. It was commendable of him. A good, good thing.

Except that should her flirtation and his interest go anywhere, it would never be anyplace permanent. She really would have liked that to have been different. She really, truly would have.

But such was life, she thought and sighed, glancing back at *her* family—her rescued dogs, her boarders, little Mickey who couldn't have weighed more than five pounds.

Storing the kibble pail and respooling the hose, Willa raised the latch on Mickey's kennel and lifted the tiny schnauzer to her chest. Taking a deep breath, she walked toward Joel.

As she had hoped, the baby's excitement at her overwhelming canine choices calmed as she zeroed in on the one within her reach. Almost within her reach. Willa was, after all, protective of her charges.

"Look, Scout," Joel said to the baby, his laughing gaze canted down at Willa. "It's a hairbrush."

"A comedian. How fun." She stepped closer, until Mickey was an arm's length from Leigh. Until the toes of Willa's work boots met the single toe of Joel's. Until her intention in coming so close was a foot shy of obvious. Joel didn't object to the invasion of his space so she stayed.

"Leigh. This is a dog. Dog." In an aside to Joel she said, "Not a hairbrush."

Leigh was captivated. "Gentle, now," Willa crooned, covering the baby's grabbing fingers with her own to guide her touch. Mickey gave Willa only one imploring glance before allowing himself to be used for instruction.

"Easy, easy," Willa nearly whispered, sliding her hand and Leigh's first over the dog's back then showing the baby the silky triangles of Mickey's ears, the black button of his nose, his tiny yet ferociously functional teeth and pink pearl tongue.

Leigh's attention was rapt. But so was Joel's. His head lowered, his gaze keen and focused and knowing. Knowing. Deeply, intimately knowing as he watched the stroking motion of her hand.

His nostrils flared and his eyes darkened and she absorbed that look, let it float and flitter like fairy dust to settle over her skin. Her body responded but, lovely as the feeling was this was neither the time nor the place. She was working and he was occupied and to explore what had just passed between them would take longer than the few minutes they had here.

So she raised her stubborn chin. "Why are you here, Joel? Not that I ever mind the company, of course. But you've never been the chatty type. And I know you don't have a dog to board."

"Actually, I was hoping to board Scout here. For the morning, anyway."

Nodding once, Willa waited to respond. Just for a moment, a moment she took for herself.

It was always this way for her with babies. And this baby was as picture-perfect as they came, with her lashes so long and her eyes so round and observant and her dimples framing a grin so wide and curious and full of life.

Somewhere Willa knew Joel was explaining about missing parents—his—and rendezvousing parents—Leigh's—and sisters spread hither and yon. His words only touched the surface of her consciousness.

"For the morning, you said?"

He twisted back the wrist beneath Leigh's bottom to view his watch. "I have a doctor's appointment at ten. I should be back by noon."

Willa considered that. "You have baby things for her? Or is this a fly-by-the-seat-of-my-pants endeavor?"

That devastatingly devouring grin again. "Her diaper bag is on your front porch. And her Exersaucer. That's all I could manage in one trip."

"Sure of yourself, aren't you?" Willa said and turned away. She settled Mickey back in his kennel then took that first step toward the rest of the morning and anything else that followed.

"Seems to run in the family," Joel remarked. When Willa frowned, he added, "That being sure thing? Never mind."

Yet when Willa held out her hands and Leigh dived without a second's hesitation, Joel turned the question on Willa. "Are *you* sure?"

And how was she to answer that? Truthfully? That she knew nothing about babies? That her limited maternal instincts had been honed on dogs?

That her infertility was not an open wound, yet the scars would always remain?

She couldn't say any of that and still expect him to give her these next two hours of bliss. And so she said the only thing she could.

"Yes."

# 2

THREE WEEKS. Three more weeks. Twenty-one days before returning to work was an option Joel would be allowed to consider. *Consider.*

He tightened his grip on the truck's steering wheel. Then rolled down his window because there didn't seem to be any air in the cab. The sky was blue, the sun was high and Joel couldn't breathe.

Funny that the department demanded he take sick leave when he wasn't even sick. This struggle to breathe had nothing to do with his lungs and everything to do with frustration. That didn't make him sick. Just like torn ligaments and muscle ground into hamburger and a bone held in place with synthetics didn't make him sick.

What made him sick was ineffectual waiting, doing nothing, twiddling his thumbs. Doc Anders wouldn't even release him to be assigned temporary desk duty.

"Not a chance, Wolf Man," the doc had answered when Joel had asked that very thing not an hour ago. "I know you too well. I let you near the station, you'll be swinging that cast like a weapon, coldcocking the first thug who looks at you crossways."

Doc had laughed then and shook his head, as if

he'd conjured an image from a bad police sitcom and inserted his dialogue into the script. "The Big Bad Wolf behind a desk? Face it. I'd last longer rolling gauze bandages than you would pushing a pencil."

Joel had mumbled and grumbled that the doc didn't know what he was talking about even though it was obvious the man had Joel's number. He shouldn't have been surprised. There wasn't a soul he knew who didn't have his number.

He was about as open as his own back door, as uncomplicated as a cup of straight black coffee. No artificial flavor or la-di-da foam mucked up the pleasure he took from caffeine. And no pretext or agenda masked the truth in his intentions.

He wanted to go back to work. Work was his life. The one thing more important to him than any other. He'd arranged his entire existence so that nothing, nothing interfered. Damn funny how when it finally happened, it was the job itself that had brought him to a grinding halt.

Joel made the slow turn from the blacktop highway onto the long road that wound back deep into the woods. This area north of Houston was quiet and isolated and still only minutes from civilization's conveniences. It was the lazy way to get back to nature; he liked the solitude, the crickets, the smell of pine.

He also liked keeping a tangible boundary between his private life and the grisly details of the day. He wasn't a fool; he was never truly off duty. But the downshift in gears was mental survival.

The minute his truck tires hit gravel he was on Wolfsley time. His home was his retreat and his sanity. This was where he unwound at the end of a shift with a cold beer, a thick steak, rare, hot off the grill and blues the way only John Lee Hooker delivered.

He enjoyed his own company; preferred to spend the evenings, when he made it home before midnight, on his back porch with the wide star-spangled sky and the furtive rustle of night creatures who shared his property and scraps of his food.

He wondered why Willa chose to live here. Her profession obviously demanded the big outdoors, the seclusion, the room for the dogs to run, to play, to do their territorial doggy thing. He doubted suburban neighbors would have tolerated the noise or the smell, not that he ever noticed either. Willa kept the place clean.

He wondered about her family. People came and went from her house and the kennels behind. They brought pets to board. They brought strays to leave. They brought children and checkbooks and left with four extra legs and a tail. He never saw anyone come and stay.

He wondered why that was. Joel thought it a shame that she spent her time alone, but that was because he was used to big hugs and running tackles and wrestling matches that became flailing piles of arms and legs and sisters and nieces and nephews. The Wolfsleys, as a rule, had no decorum.

Of course not everyone was as loose with their affection. Which was the biggest damn shame of all. As far as Joel was concerned, there wasn't a man, a woman, a child alive who couldn't use a fraction of the Wolfsleys' whole.

But most of all, he wondered why he never saw Willa with a man. She was a damn good-looking woman. Tall and fit, she rarely wore makeup—or at least none visible to his untrained male eye. Her skin was creamy and lightly freckled. He guessed that's what he noticed most, that bit of copper dusting the bridge of her nose and cheekbones.

Golden-blond hair, shoulder-blade length, was always pulled back in a band, at least the strands she didn't fight to keep tamed. Her blue eyes flashed, flirted and gave him fits long after they'd talked at their respective mailboxes or exchanged hellos across the line of brush and trees that ran the length of their joint property line.

He thought too often about how her eyes would look in the dark, what it would be like to watch from above as they widened, fluttered, grew stormy and glazed. He thought of…other things as well. Things like watching her freckles flush, dampening her skin, replacing the cloth band at her nape with a ring of sweet sweat that soaked into her hair.

Joel groaned. *Nice going, Wolf Man.* Like sitting in this seat with a stiff leg wasn't bad enough. He eased his thoughts from imagined specifics to safe generalities, eased his body into less of a bind. So what if Willa starred in his private thoughts?

He wasn't into nameless, faceless body parts, or slick magazine pages of available skin. He liked to put a name to his fantasies. His thoughts were just a natural progression, the way the wind of mutual flirtation blew.

It wasn't like he was a pervert, sitting naked on his deck in the dark, staring at the light in her windows, hoping to catch a glimpse…

*Enough.* He turned off the fantasy and into his drive. Wondering how Leigh had fared this morning, he steered his truck on past his house and up beneath the carport attached to the garage he'd long since converted. Half now functioned as a workroom, the other half a gym.

Ah, well. Time to fetch the munchkin. And since it appeared he was going to be munchkin-sitting for the week, it was time to shop. Jen had left diapers and wipes and formula and food, but only enough for one evening because one evening was supposed to have been the extent of Leigh's visit. Joel wasn't prepared or supplied for seven days.

Because walking was a pain and it was a long way from the back of his driveway to the front entrance to Willa's place, he cut through the stand of brush and pines separating his yard from hers.

The short walk put him at her back door. He braced his weight on his cane, hobbled up the two steps and knocked. A minute later she answered.

A minute after that he concluded that no wet T-shirt he'd seen held the appeal of the dry white tank top Willa wore. She hadn't been wearing it this morning, or if she had he hadn't noticed. And that was not very likely, even though this morning he'd been mesmerized by her hands.

She'd held that tiny hairbrush of a dog in strong female fingers, stroked the fur with sure movements, taken Leigh's tiny palm and patiently introduced baby to dog in low, calm, soothing tones.

Nothing about Willa's touch or voice had been sexual or arousing. Still, his blood had been stirred.

Now he stood on the second step of three and Willa stood a head above in the doorway to her kitchen. She was a tall woman but he was taller still. His height and her height and that second step/third step combination put him eye-level with her chest, where ribbed cotton molded full breasts, where dark centers peaked against light material.

He forced his gaze higher but that wasn't any better because she had these shoulders that were sensuously muscled and rounded and set back at a confident angle. He'd never noticed her strength before, a strength of health and softness and gentle feminine curves. And, yes, that stirred him, too.

She was a woman and he was a man. He was going to look, to appreciate and enjoy what she'd so obviously been blessed with physically. What he wasn't going to do was embarrass Willa or, worse, himself.

He swallowed hard, wiped his palms against his jeans and looked up into her eyes.... Breathing would've been easier if the expression he encountered hadn't seemed to be an invitation. To look. At will.

He couldn't find his voice. He almost couldn't move. He certainly couldn't manage anything right then beyond keeping his balance there on the steps.

"I had to change." She gave a small shrug in punctuation, and reached for a shirt lying on the counter closest to the door. When she looked his way again, her curves were draped in green and blue flannel and every hint of "what if" was gone.

He was relieved and annoyed, but most of all confused by what just had or had not happened. Had not, most likely. He shook off what his imagination and restlessness had no doubt conjured out of thin air. An invitation. Right. He was really reaching if he believed that one.

"Don't tell me," he said, glad to hear the words coming from his mouth. "Leigh did that hawk-and-spit thing with her breakfast."

Chuckling in that low soft way she had, Willa motioned him up the final step and inside. "The spitting I can see, but she's a bit too young to have figured out the hawking part. But not to worry. It wasn't Leigh. Just a very scared, very muddy, very strong dog."

She closed the door behind Joel. Sunlight beamed through the crystal panes of the door's inset window that remained curtain free. The light shone gold on her exposed skin, glinted off random strands of gilt-colored hair that refused the band at the back of her head. Her ponytail was thick and rich and Joel was obviously out of his mind for letting his thoughts stray.

This wasn't like him. Sure he got flustered and bothered at inappropriate times. He was a man. A man who lived alone, worked long hours and had a social life the size of a flea. But this was Willa. His neighbor. Willa Grace Darling.

And because she'd become his most recent fantasy, that bothered and flustered him most. "Trust me. It won't be long. She has a couple of older nephews who think spitting contests rank right up there with belching."

"I'll have to take your word for that." Motioning Joel to take a seat at the rectangular pine table, Willa returned to the coffeemaker, added eight cups of water and flipped the switch to Brew. "There's a huge gap in my education when it comes to frogs and snails and puppy dog tails."

"Easy lesson." Joel pulled out a chair, hooked his cane on the chair back, sat and eased his *sick* leg straight out in front of him. Then he glanced around.

This was the first time he'd seen Willa's kitchen, or any of her house for that matter. He liked what he saw. Clean and uncluttered and Amish plain. White cabinets and white tile countertops and stainless-steel sink. Much like his place. A guy's kitchen.

Except for the row of tiny clay pots in her windowsill. Pots with enough greenery to color more than one thumb. Bushy leaves and trailing leaves, tiny fronds that dangled almost to the sink and climbing vines that reached for the sky.

"Part one," he continued after he'd settled and decided that several of the plants were herbs. "When it comes to boys, the more ooze and goo and mess the better. And, part two, when you can buy it prepackaged in neon colors as advertised on cable TV...hey, who needs mud pies and swamp things?"

"You sound like a man who knows his way around children." She'd turned to face him, her back against the counter's edge, her arms crossed over her middle. Steam rose from the coffeemaker in rich spurts and fragrant gurgles.

He'd been wrong. The flannel didn't cover her curves at all. He inhaled and savored the aroma of dark coffee almost as much as the picture Willa made there. "Only the Wolfsley children. Carolyn, sister number two," he held up two fingers, "has three boys, six, eight and ten, and Jen's husband, Rob, has a son who's nine. I think."

"You think," she reiterated.

"Hey, I've got a lot to keep up with here. Moira, that's sister number three," he added another finger, "has a daughter she's raising alone. If not for Laura, poor Leigh wouldn't have anyone to side with her in the battle of the sexes."

Slowly, as slow as the smile that formed on her mouth, Willa turned, reaching high to pull mugs from the cupboard. Her arms were longer than Joel had realized. As was her back from her nape to her hips where her blue jeans rode low.

A strip of skin peeked between her waistband and the hem of her flannel and Joel discovered a sudden interest in the pattern of the pine tabletop. He continued that study until Willa set a plain white ceramic mug filled with black coffee between his hands. For a moment he stared at the line where the black met the white.

When at last he looked up, she was still standing against the counter smiling. "I didn't know you had sisters, Joel. I've lived next door to you for a year now and I didn't know that about you."

A year, huh? Joel wasn't sure if he was ruing his mistake of not getting to know her then, or the sudden certainty that he was going to get to know her now. That he was going to get to know her well. That he was going to get to know her soon and more intimately than any fantasy he'd concocted so far.

"So how did you know I took my coffee black?" he asked as she moved to sit in the chair across from his.

Her booted foot bumped his cast and she grimaced in apology. "You look like a black coffee kinda guy. Straightforward and all that."

Interesting she'd gauged that when they'd never had a conversation of more than five or six paragraphs. His expression must have been as easy to read as he apparently always was because she lowered her mug without sipping.

"It's a simple observation, Joel. You needed a sitter. You didn't beat around the bush. You came and asked me. Like I said, straightforward."

"And all that," he added. She inclined her head in a silent *touché*.

Okay. He could deal with her assessment; first of all because she was right. He *was* a black coffee kinda guy. And, secondly, she seemed equally candid. He liked that about her. "How's Leigh?"

"Leigh's been a doll. No mess but for a diaper or two." She took that sip of coffee, then raised one hand as a thought crossed her mind. "In fact, she slept through the whole commotion."

"Commotion?" His ears pricked. Finally. A distraction up his alley. "What commotion?"

"Relax, Detective. Nothing of the law-and-order variety." She smiled again. Good cheer and good humor and good nature combined in one sweet upward curve of her mouth. That smile reached all the way to her eyes. And all the way to his hunger. His gut was a mess.

But, those eyes. Her eyes were going to be the death of him. "Let me guess. If not the law-and-order variety, it must've been canine. The scared and muddy and very strong canine."

As slowly as that expression had brightened her face earlier, it now began a slow fade, darkening and growing grim. The morning's ordeal, whatever it was, hadn't left her unshaken.

When she sighed, the sound spoke volumes. He waited for her to gather her thoughts, waited for her voice. Waited for anything that would give him a clue as to why his reaction to her was so far out of context as to be out of line.

She strolled a finger around the rim of her mug, dipped the tip close to the coffee she'd flavored and sweetened. Then she placed both hands flat on the table, leaned forward with a sense of urgency and very succinctly enunciated, "I do not understand people."

It was a broad comment, but Joel knew exactly what she meant. Several clever comments came to mind that he decided not to voice. He wanted her to go on. He found he liked her voice as much as her tendency to say what she was thinking.

"What happened?" he gently prodded.

She blinked and glanced first at her mug then looked up, cocked her head to one side and met his steady gaze. "You would think that humans would be inherently humane. But I suppose the Latin root doesn't always apply."

"You're right. It doesn't," he said and sat back. "If it did my job would be a lot easier."

"Oh, yes. Yours even more so than mine." She nodded then shook her head, moving from one thought to the next. "What happened today happens too often. And right about this time of year. Once owners come to realize that Christmas puppies aren't quite so cute and cuddly four months later."

She lifted her mug, stared out the back window. "This one had been randomly fed and regularly beaten. It's a laugh riot when a cartoon Dalmatian plays tug-o'-war with an old shoe. Not quite so funny when you're running late for work and finally find your missing two-hundred-dollar Ferragamo flats in three pieces."

She didn't seem to be in the mood for a joke, but humor had always worked with his sisters. "I'll take a stab that a Ferragamo flat is a shoe."

"A two-hundred dollar shoe." She frowned. "A one-hundred dollar shoe if you want to get divisive, but since one is no good without the other, I'm afraid it's the pair that has to be depreciated."

"You own a pair of these…flats?" Sounded like a tire. He'd thought so ever since Moira had slapped around the family kitchen in a five-sizes-too-big pair that belonged to their mother. Her footsteps had sounded just like a flat tire.

"Me?" Willa leaned back in her chair, swung her leg up and around and plopped her foot on the corner of the table. "Waterproof, oiled split leather. Padded tongue. Steel shank. Air-cushion midsole. Molded rubber heel protector. These—" she pointed her toe, managing to make the chunky boots seem feminine, "—these are *worth* two hundred dollars."

He couldn't resist. He twisted to the side in his chair, lifted his leg and balanced the heel of his cast on the very edge of the table. He wasn't totally uncouth. "I've got you beat. This is worth…hmm, I've lost count."

Returning her chair to rights, Willa sipped her coffee, staring into his eyes as she did so. Hers were blue. Not baby blue or navy blue or even that peacock turquoise that ninety-nine percent of the time owed its color to contact lenses.

No, this was the blue of clear water, of the sky at high noon. Corny sounding, he knew. But her eyes appeared to be lit from within. She had that type of energy. He'd seen the proof in the way she ran her place, from dawn to dusk.

Reaching across the table, she tapped his exposed toes with one finger. "Line of duty?"

He nodded, because he hadn't yet let go of her eyes. And because a tickle was working its way up his foot, his calf, his knee…he squashed it before it climbed higher. "Yep. Line of duty."

"Then I'm sure the department considers it money well spent."

"They haven't seen the final bill. This puppy doesn't come off for three more weeks." He raised his cast and returned his foot to the floor.

"And once it's off?"

"Physical therapy for sure. I'm not about to go back on the street without being in top form."

She frowned. "Was there a lot of damage?"

"Enough." He didn't want to spell out every gory detail. "It wasn't pretty."

"A bullet?"

"To start with. It grazed my calf. Plowed quite a

row through the muscle. Most of the damage happened when the shooter ran...and tried to take me out with his car. I dived but he clipped my leg as I went down."

The pain returned, a memory that was but a moment yet played out like a slow-motion film. Funny how when he thought of the incident now, he saw the gun come up, saw his body go down, saw the car lay rubber in its flight. He even saw, rather than felt, the smashing impact of the bumper against his shin.

He shook his head, swallowed his coffee, held his mug against the table. Then looked up at Willa. If he'd thought her eyes were bright before, they shimmered now. And the jolt they packed this time hit him square in the chest.

"Hey, now, don't go making me out a hero. It's just part of the job. Like dealing with scared and muddy puppies is part of what you do." He reached across the table, placed her hand, palm up, in his, and pushed the sleeve of her flannel to her elbow. That gave him access to the scratches crisscrossing her wrist and forearm in a tic-tac-toe welt.

He hadn't expected that her skin would be as soft as Leigh's. For all the work she did outdoors, the work that put those muscles in her arms and shoulders, her skin remained that of a woman who rarely saw the sun and certainly never battled a clawing canine.

The salve on her wounds hadn't been absorbed completely. He thumbed a smear of the clear substance into her palm, swirled it in a slow circle over the heel of her hand, drew it in a line along the base of her fingers, pressed the pad of his thumb to her pulse.

He measured each beat, found the rhythm in sync with the blood in his veins. He took a deep breath. Arousal moved from his body to his brain, burying the warnings of playing with fire beneath thoughts of the pleasure of getting burned.

Willa cleared her throat.

Joel jumped. What the hell was he doing? "You need to see a doctor for this?"

She shook her head, but left her hand where it rested in his. "All my shots are up to date. Just like the dogs I keep here."

"The rescued dogs, too?"

"If I don't know for certain and have no way to find out, they get the full battery before they even get a bath. No need to calm them once only to have to do it all over again."

He nodded at that, then pulled his hand from beneath hers so he could finish his coffee even though he already had one free hand perfectly capable of lifting mug to mouth.

When he'd swallowed the last drop and there was really no reason to stay longer, no reason that made sense or possessed a shred of logic, he scooted back his chair and prepared to go. "I'd better grab Scout and hit the road."

"Taking her home?"

He couldn't keep the irony from his laugh. Last night's series of phone calls to track down his parents was Marx Brothers comical in retrospect. "Only to *my* home. Jennifer dropped off Leigh last night on the way to the airport. I was going to keep her until our folks got home."

"Uh-oh."

"Uh-oh is right. Seems Mom and Dad got a wild hair and took off for LA to see Annie."

"Sister number four?"

He nodded. "That would be her."

"When is Jennifer due back?"

"Next Sunday."

"Uh-oh," she said again. Her expression was contemplative, then she added, "What're you going to do?"

He shrugged then smiled when he heard Leigh giggle. "Take care of that munchkin in there until her momma gets home."

Leaving him with a look that strangely enough seemed an expression of pleasure, Willa was out of her chair before Joel could find his balance, retrieve his cane and lever his butt out of his seat. She hadn't even given his uncle instincts a chance to kick in, but had gone for Scout herself. Another thing he liked. Her take-charge confidence.

He watched her walk away. Enjoyed the curvy rear and lower view as much as he had the rest of Willa Darling. He smiled at the built-in endearment of her name, words that gave the impression of a gentle feminine soul. He was sure she was just that, exactly, and more.

The more was what intrigued him now. The more he hadn't witnessed until today, even having been aware that this very beautiful woman lived next door.

*Aware.* That was what he found so amazing. In the space of half a day he was so aware of Willa that his blood was surging, his nerves humming, his body alive and willing in a way it hadn't been for longer than he cared to remember.

His loner status didn't mean he was celibate, but neither did he play games or engage in intimacies without thought. The women he'd chosen to spend time with in the past had chosen him for much the same reason. They provided one another with companionship and met one another's physical needs, no long-term expectations.

He'd been without a woman for a while now, except for the one in his fantasies.

He missed the warmth, the softness, the sweet and sweaty smells. He missed laughter as much as low throaty moans. He missed exerting control as well as having the same wrested away. He had no problem with either surrender or aggression as long as mutual satisfaction resulted.

Thinking about Willa and satisfaction began a stirring that Joel tamped down. It was a useless expending of energy. He couldn't see having an affair with Willa when she lived next door, and would still live next door once any relationship they might have was over.

And it would be over. That was the promise he'd made himself when he'd sworn the bigger oath to serve and protect. Of course this whole train of thought was ridiculous.

But the fact that he was having such thought at all proved that he desperately needed to get back to work before he did something stupid.

Like seducing his neighbor.

# 3

"HEY, SWEETIE." Willa lifted the waking baby from the pallet on the floor in the front room where Leigh had slept for close to an hour. Gordy got to his feet as well, stretching first in forward then in reverse.

The dog had spent Leigh's nap time on self-appointed, border-collie guard duty four feet away. Now he padded behind Willa toward the couch, his short nails clicking on the hardwood floor. When she sat, he sat, taking up position near the cushion where Willa placed the baby.

"Good dog. Good dog." She rewarded her loyal friend with a scratch behind his ears then reached for Leigh's diaper bag. Changing time. Leigh rubbed her fists in her eyes then stared up at Willa.

This baby was a heartbreaker. Even a heart as pliable as Willa's wasn't immune to those big Bambi-browns. "You had a nice long nap, didn't you, Sweetie?"

Earlier in the day, Leigh had accompanied Willa to the kennel area at the back of the wooded lot. From beneath the shade of tall, tall pines, the toes of her white shoes scuffing at the carpet of green needles, the baby had watched from her Exersaucer with rapt interest while Willa tended to the rescued dogs.

She'd listened to the soothing tones Willa used to calm the most frightened and fragile of the animals. Watched and listened until the combination of the sun's warmth filtered by pine boughs and the soft breeze had her chin bobbing against her chest, her long lashes brushing her cheeks. A whisper of air had lifted her white-blond curls like gossamer ribbons on angel wings.

And Willa's heart had swelled. She'd lifted the baby from the saucer seat and cradled her close.

Once inside, she'd spread a layer of thick blankets on the hardwood floor of the cottage's front room, managing to do it with one hand. She'd been uncomfortable with the idea of leaving the little sleepyhead alone, tucked deep into the sofa cushions of blue and white ticking, while she finished with the dogs.

And she couldn't leave Leigh in the back of the house, her knees drawn up beneath her tummy, her diapered bottom in the air, to sleep in the bed in the one big room that served as Willa's personal sanctuary. Not that Leigh wouldn't have loved the thick comforter and decadent mountain of pillows as much as Willa did. Of course she would have. What girl wouldn't? But the gauze panels hanging from the black iron canopy bed might present a dangerous temptation to a curious baby rousing from a nice nap.

In the end, the pallet had been a sanity-saving stroke of genius. It put Willa within easy hearing distance of the baby's sweet waking noises, coos and giggles. She'd used those noises as a legitimate excuse to escape the table in the kitchen and the look in the Big Bad Wolf's eyes.

*The better to see you with, my dear.*

She shivered and struggled longer than she should have with the tapes on Leigh's diaper, though the way the baby was twisting to reach for Gordy's snout required uncommon dexterity to begin with. Still, Willa had to be honest with herself. The baby's antics had little to do with her inability to focus, to shake the kitchen scene from moments ago.

Willa had an excellent sense of recall. And the way Joel had studied her then, sitting across the table from her there, was unforgettable. It was as if pages of thoughts had opened like a book, as if every word that had run through his mind had been spelled out in text beneath those gloriously thick lashes.

It was as if he had wanted her to read him, to know he was thinking about wanting her. Oh, the things she'd seen written behind those eyes so green—words lush and erotic and seductive and raw. Words whose meanings she understood in her mind, and *felt* in her body—deeply, fully in her body.

Willa knew she had a different sort of "look," one that many men liked. She'd never cultivated it particularly, but the work she did was physical, requiring a strength and stamina of the type that built muscles. And she was tall. Not Amazon-size, but eye level with the average man.

Joel was not average. The way he looked at her wasn't average at all. At least not average in her experience of dealing with men. Most considered her ballsy because she spoke her mind instead of pulling shrinking-violet punches. But she'd never equated her femininity with her personality.

She knew, without vanity, that her femininity was inherent in her walk, in the way her long legs carried her fluidly and the way her hips rolled.

It was in her tender care, the way she intuitively sensed the needs of others and ministered in the fashion that only a woman could.

It came with her sensuality, her awareness of all around her and the rich joy in her body's response to the rare man whose passion and intelligence and sense of humor elicited such.

That latter combination drew her in every time. And every time she had to be careful because those were the men born to mate forever—to pass on their love of life to children born of their loins.

The forever part was her dream. One day she'd find it. But because she couldn't provide any man with children, she'd come to the realization that her forever might take longer to find than she wanted.

"Okay, Sweetie," she said, arranging the baby's rumpled dress over her freshly changed and padded bottom. Willa got to her feet, lifting Joel's now wide-awake munchkin to her hip as she did. "Let's see what Uncle Joel thinks about finding you some lunch."

"Uncle Joel can't think of anything he'd rather do right now."

His voice held the same decadent temptation as dark chocolate. Why, oh why, did she have such a hard time saying no? She turned to find Joel leaning against the archway that opened to the kitchen.

She didn't doubt he hungered for lunch, but the

way he stood, the way his eyes devoured her, told Willa that he sensed and shared the turbulence that had propelled her out of the kitchen minutes ago.

He had listened to the words she hadn't spoken. Known what she'd intended to say with the ones she had. He was listening now. She knew it. And she tried so very hard to still her thoughts.

*The better to hear you with, my dear.*

Ha! What good would it do to still her thoughts when he could surely hear her pulse racing, the thud of her heart in her chest, the wild battle being fought between emotion and intellect?

She hadn't been prepared for this when she'd looked up this morning to see him making his laborious way across her yard, a darling baby's arm around his neck. He was her neighbor, the cop, the Big Bad Wolf next door. She had to keep this attraction in perspective.

"However," Joel said, intruding on Willa's thoughts as he walked into the front room. "Finding the munchkin some lunch is going to require a trip to the store. Jen only left enough food for last night. Lucky for Leigh there was a box of instant cereal in the bottom of her bag. That took care of this morning. But we're up a creek now. I have a fridge full of steaks and burgers and that's about it."

Having caught sight of her uncle, Leigh let out a happy squeal and reached for him with both arms. Willa made her way to where Joel stood and surrendered the precious armful. Once Leigh settled her head against Joel's shoulder Willa stroked the baby's hair. The blond curls sifted through her fingers like strands of fine silk.

"I'm not much help in the food department." Willa crossed her arms, missing the comfortable weight of the baby, still smelling the scent that was a baby's alone and Leigh's in particular. "I think I have one artichoke and a quart bowl of black bean soup."

Joel grimaced. "Ugh. You'd better come with us."

The suggestion had been on the tip of her tongue, but having Joel ask brought a smile. As did his obvious male disgust with anything vegetarian. "I'm fine with the food, but I thought you might need help managing the logistics of the trip. Do you have a car seat?"

Joel blew out a frustrated sigh, shoved his free hand over his forehead and back through his thicket of hair. "That would look good, wouldn't it? Getting ticketed in my own neighborhood. Jen is gonna owe me big-time when she gets home."

Willa kept her mouth in a straight line though the effort was not a battle, but an entire war. His soft spot was enormous, as vast as the extent of her love for the animals who shared her home. Joel was truly an attractive man. A Big Bad Wolf with such big teeth and so little bite.

*The better to eat you with, my dear.*

He shifted the squirming Leigh to the other arm and Willa suppressed her take-over tendencies along with a rush of blood that sang through her veins. The baby had spotted Gordy who had moved to sit at Willa's feet. But dealing with his niece was Joel's call. Not hers.

"Hey, Scout." Joel bounced the baby against his hip. "That pup's not used to you like Shadow is.

You get hold of him he's liable to get hold of you right back."

But the baby wouldn't stop twisting and turning and seconds later added a vocal protest. A very loud vocal protest. Willa didn't want to challenge what Joel thought best, but she did know her dog.

"He's very gentle." She spoke quietly, rubbing behind the dog's ears as she continued. "He doesn't have the energy or the inclination to be anything else. He ran his heart out until a couple of years ago when he decided to retire. He's been my right-hand man ever since."

Joel's eyes twinkled like dew on morning grass. "Retired, did he?"

She nodded, sinking down to her haunches next to the dog who nuzzled her shoulder with his head. "Now he helps me out when he's not busy entertaining small children." She lifted her gaze to Joel's face, asking for his trust. "That's his biggest joy, you know."

"No. I didn't know," he answered, and when Willa reached up he lowered the anxious baby. Their hands met, hers over his beneath Leigh's outstretched arms. His skin was warm and electrically charged, as it had been when he'd held her hand in the kitchen, when he'd pressed his thumb to the pulse in her wrist.

He gave up the baby to Willa's keeping and eased down to the floor, his back against the curve of the archway. One leg he stretched out in front of him, the other knee he drew up and used to rest his wrist.

His hand dangled there, his fingers long, his hand wide with prominent veins and a sprinkling of golden hair that grew thicker over forearms defined with muscle.

Willa experienced a sweet urge to touch his hand as he'd held hers earlier. To explore further—the pads of his fingers, the width of his knuckles, the breadth of his palm and the shape of his nails.

To feel more than the touch of his hand in return. A continuation of the touch he'd begun there in the kitchen. The wanting was sensual more than sexual, yet the thought lingered. Lingered.

Denying a shiver, Willa sat cross-legged, hugged Leigh to her side. At the pat of Willa's hand on the floor, Gordy padded over to the spot. When she clicked her fingers, he sat and awaited further orders.

Joel shook his head. "Nicely done. Think you can teach me that trick. I could use it with Leigh this week."

It was rubbing up against her again. That sensation of something so right. Purring and insistent in that way her female intuition worked. There was a chance here worth taking, a chance she needed to allow herself to take.

But first things first. "Well, it was six or eight months before Gordy and I were on the same wavelength." She scratched beneath the dog's chin. "From what I understand that doesn't happen between parents and children until…eighteen? Nineteen? Twenty-five?"

The quirk of Joel's mouth was a knowing one. "Sometimes as late as thirty."

"And sometimes never," Willa added automatically, keeping her eye on tiny fingers tentatively exploring the dog's face. She and her parents had yet to reach the same wavelength. A situation that deteriorated each year she remained single.

They'd never come to terms with her inability to bear children. The fall, the surgery…to this day they hadn't admitted that no one was at fault. That no one deserved the blame. That accidents did happen.

Their insistence on taming their tomboy in an exorcism of ruffles and bows and patent leather had sent Willa scrambling up towering trees, mad-dashing down gullies, squeezing into drain pipes, pole vaulting over fences…and then, the damage was done.

Willa had come to terms with her injuries early on. The tomboy in her had worn the scars like a warrior. She was a warrior still. And the woman she'd become knew she hadn't lost her worth that day long ago. She was sad that her parents thought it so. No, they were not on the same wavelength at all.

A smile tickled its way across Willa's mouth. She felt the curve of her lips and let it go. Oh, how her parents would love her to land a man like Joel Wolfsley.

And oh, how she loved his laugh. A deep male rumbling that spoke of good humor and good nature and did good things to that determined tickle low in Willa's belly.

"'Never' is probably way too accurate," he said, picking up her train of thought. "I think that's called the generation gap. I see it every time the Wolfsleys get together. The kids speak a language foreign to everyone but each other.

"And half the time I'm not sure I understand

what my folks are talking about." The green in his eyes twinkled with affection. "But then they've had their own language for forty years now."

Willa watched Joel's light show of emotions, the shake of his head, the quirk of his lips, the mesh of lines at the corners of his eyes. The combination was explosively engaging. As was his appreciation of what his parents shared.

She wondered what a relationship like that, for so long, years and years, would mean to a person's life. She wondered if Joel had a similar wish for his future.

And then she poked around to see if a shred of wanting something similar for herself remained. It did, but the spot wasn't as tender as it had been the last time she checked. She liked that. It was a good sign that her life was her own and that she was happy.

"You do that a lot? Get together?"

Joel made sure Leigh's curiosity about Gordy's teeth didn't cost her a finger. "Not a lot. The usual occasions. Christmas. Thanksgiving. Those are the times everyone shows. Whoever can makes it to the rest. Memorial Day. July Fourth. We try to do something on our folks' birthdays but it's hit or miss."

Leigh was now planting big sloppy kisses on the long-suffering dog's snout. Gordy turned imploring eyes to Willa and blinked. She moved the baby to sit in the cradle of her lap and her dog smiled. "How often do you have your family out to your place?"

"Me?" He poked his thumb at his chest. "The

guy with nothing in his fridge but steaks and burger and stock in Royal Oak charcoal?"

"Sure. Why not? July Fourth is a perfect canvas for your Royal Oak skills."

He frowned, removed Gordy's ear from Leigh's fist and tweaked his niece's nose. She slapped at his hand with both of hers. "I pitch in when we cook out. Macho-man cooking, you know," he added and flexed a biceps until the muscle bulged against his T-shirt in a most mouthwatering display. "I just don't do it out here. At my place."

"Why not? You have the space and privacy, room for the kids' spitting contest." She was truly curious, as curious as Leigh had become with the way Gordy lifted his tail every time she reached for it. Baby giggles filled the silence that was less tense than somber. Thoughtful.

Joel made a grimace. "It's hard to explain. But I figure, I have two lives. One on-duty. One off. And I try not to let the first pollute the second."

"Is this a Jekyll and Hyde thing?"

He wiggled both brows like a mad scientist. "You see the movie *I Was A Teenage Werewolf*?"

It was a terrible image that came to mind and she laughed. "Then the rumors I hear of Detective Joel Wolfsley are true. The Big Bad Wolf lives up to his name."

"Well, yeah. I do." He looked into her eyes as he said it. And though a remnant of a smile remained and a glimmer of "Aw, shucks," sparkled with Huck Finn innocence, there was no mistaking the ferocity of the Big Bad Wolf.

Or the willingness to use deadly force by the man who bore the name.

Comprehension dawned. But she let the silliness ride. "That's why you don't have the family Fourth of July at your place. Because you might mutate. Or forget to shave."

This time he tweaked Willa's nose. "It runs deeper than that, but, yeah, that's the nutshell version."

"What's the rest of it?" she asked, knowing she had no right to pry and that he certainly had no reason to trust her with such a confidence. He'd made his life decisions just as she'd made hers.

But he had just tweaked her nose. An intimately playful gesture that showed they'd reached a fair level of comfort. He might not answer, but she'd had to ask.

"I don't think I've ever told anyone the rest of it. They've picked up on the obvious." He straightened the other leg, crossed his good ankle over the bad, crossed his arms high on his chest, tucked his fingers in his armpits. "But then it doesn't take a rocket scientist to figure there's a danger factor in what I do for a living."

"Not to your family, surely?" she asked, then considered his posture and his protective instincts. "But there is, isn't there? A danger."

He shook his head. "Not now. There has been. In the past. A couple of creeps have made lame threats involving the females in my family." He paused, moving to take Leigh's tiny hand in his own, cupping her chin, looking into her eyes and dropping a kiss onto the button of her nose.

When he spoke, his voice was low, deep—a growl that rumbled up from the back of his throat.

He leaned closer, into Willa's space. "There are a lot of females in my family, Willa."

She didn't know what to say. She barely managed to take a breath. He was a hunter, protector, leader of the pack. Bold, brash, arrogant. And dangerous. Oh so incredibly dangerous.

He was a man unlike any she'd met. Her intuition and instincts and female heart wanted to know him better. "And you want to keep them safe."

His smile had the look of the devil himself. "I *will* keep them safe."

Willa drew in a huge breath. "Well, Detective Wolfsley. The females in your family are fortunate women."

He huffed at that and the tension vanished. Smoke in the air. "Ask any one of them and they'll say they're smothered, stifled, perfectly capable of looking out for themselves…and that's just what they say to my face. No telling what they really think."

"I know what they really think," she said and grinned.

Joel frowned. "Uh-oh. This is one of those female things, isn't it? Like going to the ladies' room in groups? Or managing to have every dish ready to eat at the same time? Or knowing you can't wear red if you have red hair?"

"You can wear red if you have red hair. You just have to be red savvy." His confusion delighted her. "But, no. This is just common sense. The fact that your sister didn't think twice about leaving this baby in your safekeeping proves what she thinks of you."

"What she *thought* of me, you mean. When she gets back and sees I've let Leigh go to the dogs, she'll probably never speak to me again. C'mere, Scout. That pup is not a pillow. Or a horse."

He reached for the baby, set her on her shaky feet. "Sorry, Willa. She's used to tumbling with Shadow who *is* a pillow and a horse."

"And lets Leigh use him for both, no doubt."

"You got that right. The finer points of pet ownership are lost on this one, I'm afraid. Oh, criminy," he muttered, lifting Leigh from her position, belly down, face flat, rump up, from the dog's back. She squealed her outrage.

He lifted her overhead, blew a fat raspberry against her tummy. Giggles erupted and spittle flew and Willa's heart filled with the beauty of the moment.

What a lucky family, these Wolfsleys. "You know, Detective. You'll make one hell of a daddy some day."

He returned Leigh to the floor, rolled his eyes when she scampered back onto Gordy's back. "Nah. I'm too old and worn out and fatherhood would send me over the edge."

"You say that now—"

"And I'll say it tomorrow and the day after. I'm the proverbial bachelor type, Willa." He spread his arms wide. "Hell, here I am, thirty-four years old and I've never had a relationship last beyond a few months. I know for a fact that a family requires a longer commitment."

"You'll make it when the time is right."

He shook his head. "I'm too selfish."

She shook hers, too. "Try and sell that elsewhere. I'm not buying."

"Okay. I'm too set in my ways. I live on steaks and burgers and beer. I don't have a single potted plant in my house. I have a job that means strange hours and stranger...strangers hanging around."

He looked incredibly convinced and proud of his reasoning when he said, "I can't think of a better definition of bachelorhood. Or a better guarantee that I'd last in a permanent relationship for about ten minutes."

She knew he was kidding himself. He had fatherhood and family written all over his face. It showed in his eyes of green meadows, in the shadow of his early-morning five-o'clock beard.

But she wasn't going to tell him that he was wrong. She didn't want him to hear the truth. Not from her. And she certainly didn't want to speak it.

Not since she'd decided she wanted to be his lover.

# 4

"YOU'RE GOING to need help."

Leaving Joel standing at the register with her pithy words and the bill in his hand, Willa carried a very messy Leigh into the ladies' room of the diner where he'd treated them to a lunch of his favorite home-style cooking.

Chicken-fried steak. Garlic potatoes and cream gravy. Hot rolls with butter and green beans with ham. Willa, of course, had ordered a salad. A spinach salad. And Leigh—criminy!

The queen of Cuisinart had squashed each bean into a pulp of green strings against the high-chair tray, mashed already mashed potatoes between her fingers, sucked a crust of bread until she'd turned it into glue and dreadlocked half the hair on her head.

And today was only day one. At least five more loomed in his future. Five days of bath time and play time and quiet time and feeding time. Sure he could manage on his own. He hadn't grown up the oldest of five and not done his fair share of babysitting. But it wouldn't be the same walk in the park he'd be able to make on two good feet.

He wouldn't complain about the laundry, though with the little bit Jen had packed and the way Leigh was going through her wardrobe, he'd be making a trip to his sister's house today for a week's worth of miniature outfits.

He wouldn't worry about adjusting his work or sleep schedule. Since he didn't have the first, he didn't have the second. His hours were pretty much adaptable to whatever Leigh required.

He wouldn't turn his nose up at diapers. Or spit and drool. Or the paste Leigh managed to make of fruits and vegetables. And cereal. And bread... though the way Scout looked a few minutes ago when Willa carried her off for a quick wash and wax did have Joel shaking his head.

How did someone so small create a mess so big?

He'd dressed Leigh this morning in the same clothes she'd worn when Jen dropped her off. His choices had been limited. It was either a repeat of the dress, or a pair of red Winnie the Pooh pajamas.

Jen had expected their folks to be home last night, not on their way to the West Coast. If those expectations had panned out, the clothing dilemma wouldn't have been one. Joel knew his mother kept a spare dresser full of clothes for the grandkids. Her emergency stash, she called it.

Emergency stash indeed.

Which reminded him. He needed to check in on Howie Jr. while at Jen's. Make sure the teen was taking care of Shadow as promised. Keeping clean and legal, as he'd sworn to Joel and the judge.

Yeah, Joel thought, his interest pricking as the ladies'-room door swung open and Willa stepped through. When he put it all together and added his bum leg...Willa was right. He was going to need help.

And damn but he liked the way she walked. Her

long legs wore blue jeans well. Her approach was confident, her line of sight locked on him. He liked that, too, that she had eyes for no one else. Gave a certain integrity to his thoughts of her that ran to the private and personal.

She made it to his side then, baby on her hip. Comfortably, naturally on her hip. A woman's hip, cocked to the side to support her cargo and curved to fit a man's hand, built to hold his weight, shaped to mate to his body. A groan rolled up from Joel's throat as Willa brushed a lock of Leigh's hair from her forehead.

"We're back," she said, smiling at her charge first, then at Joel. "And only a little worse for the wear."

"So, I see," he said and cleared his throat. He looked first at Leigh then at Willa. From damp blond curls to wild golden strands. He straightened where he stood. From scrubbed rosy cheeks to skin kissed with freckles. He took a step back.

From innocent Bambi-browns to intelligent eyes—eyes that knew his thoughts hovered on the verge of a proposition. He swallowed hard. It was all he could do to ask, "Ready?"

Willa nodded, and Joel pushed open the door. The sunlight hit them square in the face. Willa pulled sunglasses from the pocket of her flannel shirt. Leigh buried her face in the crook of Willa's neck. Joel kept his mind on nothing but the trip to the truck.

The breeze was cool yet the sun was hot, beating down hard enough that Joel's cane pressed into the newly tarred parking lot as he hobbled along behind them, feeling worn and old when he knew he was neither.

Worn and old was a state of mind and body that was temporary; one easily attributed to the past few weeks of doing nothing. It was a situational frustration he could deal with. Had been dealing with. Would continue to deal with.

And it was a lot easier to manage than the sensation that he'd stepped off into a great big hole when he'd crossed Willa's backyard this morning. A hole down which he was still falling, falling hard, falling deep.

He didn't like the dreamlike feeling, the loss of power over mind and body. Yeah, he'd been thinking about Willa in ways that had him knotted and stiff. But the feeling of head over heels down the side of a cliff cut a little too close to a loss of control. And that wasn't going to happen. No matter how much he wanted her.

Once at the truck, he took Leigh from Willa's arms and buckled her into the car seat that Willa had borrowed from the Craigs across the street. He had no idea how she'd known they kept one on hand for their grandbaby's visits. But she had.

There'd been a lot of things Willa had surprised him with today, he thought, watching over the top of the car seat and through the rear window as she circled the back of the truck. Her ease at handling Leigh's needs was the first.

The woman knew every in and out of babysitting. Leigh had but to babble in that baby-babble way she had and Willa's maternal instincts kicked right in—as if she'd been waiting for this opportunity.

Truth is, she hadn't been waiting for a thing. He knew that. This opportunity was just a chance for Willa to do what came naturally. Of that, he was sure. The same way he was sure there was a reason she had no children of her own. And a reason she wasn't married. Or involved.

Joel huffed, impatient with himself and his thoughts. Even though he wanted to know what it was that made Willa tick, her personal life was none of his business. Just as his was none of hers.

Of course, that hadn't stopped him from spilling most all of his guts through his big mouth at her simple prompting. *Nice going there, too, Wolf Man. Way to keep a poker face.* He would've thought he'd been on the job long enough to play the right cards in an interrogation.

Now if he could just hold on to his precarious hand for the rest of the week… Hell, he'd be happy to make it through the day, because Willa's offer to help was never out of his mind. And he wasn't yet sure his idea of help was what she had intended.

Willa climbed into the passenger side and slammed the door. Joel got behind the wheel, slid his cane across the floor, lay his arm along the top of the seat and looked over his shoulder to back out of the parking spot.

That his fingers grazed Willa's nape, grazed and tangled in loose strands of her hair, didn't faze him. Not at all. Leigh's hair was as soft. Jen's hair was as soft. His own wasn't much coarser. Just shorter. Hair was hair, after all, he reasoned, rubbing Willa's between his forefinger and thumb.

But not this time, he had to admit. And not this hair. The threads wound around his fingers on their own, alive with a static attraction drawn from Willa's energy. He breathed in and fell a little deeper. Breathed out and continued to fall.

"Sorry," she said, reaching back to bind the strands once again. "My hair has a mind of its own at times."

She smiled at him and once he'd recovered from that and had the truck heading out of the lot, he moved his arm from the back of the seat. Reluctantly.

"I keep thinking I should cut it," she said, still struggling with the cloth band that bound it in a ponytail. "It's too long to be practical."

He glanced over at her. She'd finished with her hair and was looking straight ahead now, one elbow braced on the door, her chin at rest in her palm. Her hair lay sleek against her head in multicolored shades of blond. He thought of corn silk. Of wheat fields. He thought he was out of his mind.

It was on the tip of his tongue to say, "No. Don't cut it." But instead he turned back to driving and asked, "Why don't you?"

She laughed. "Vanity, of course."

"Vanity." He grunted, an annoying noise he figured would draw a reaction. Anything to keep her talking. He intended to know her well before she stopped. "Females. I should've known."

"Now, Detective Wolfsley. What could you possibly have against females?"

"I spent eighteen years growing up with four sisters in a house that had only two bathrooms." Again a grunt. For good measure. "Women and mirrors and showers—"

"Oh, my!" Willa laughed and turned to the side to look at him while she talked. "C'mon, Joel. Think about it."

"Think about what?"

"Boys have all the fun with their frogs and snails and puppy-dog tails—"

"Damn straight," he interjected.

She cleared her throat. "And girls get stuck with sugar and spice and orders not to get dirty. We don't even have a say in the matter. It's all decided by the time we're wrapped up in the hospital nursery's one-size-fits-all pink blanket."

She'd obviously been pampered and petted, put on a pedestal, a look-but-don't-touch pretty package. He wanted to know more—who she was, her likes and dislikes. He wanted a palette to work with. Seduction was a fine art, after all. "Should've asked the nurses for blue, I guess."

She screwed up her nose, pressed her lips together in thought. "I think I would've chosen red, actually. Deep and rich and dark. Fit for tribal queens and ladies of the evening and divas and pro basketball players."

"Jen did Leigh's nursery in red and purple." Hmm. Why did *that* bit of information feel like an attempt to score points rather than another question to draw her out?

"Red and purple? Really?"

He nodded. "Rob still gripes that the room looks like a sixties' peace rally. And Jen keeps lecturing him on primary colors and child development and some psychological connection which went in one of my ears and out the other."

"Good for her. And bad for you." Willa leaned

into Leigh's car seat as Joel made a right turn. "I like your sister, Joel. This little one may be wearing white ruffles today, but she'll no doubt be decked out in soccer cleats and a goalie shirt tomorrow."

Another twist. And, vanity or not, Joel knew this was about more than clothes. There had been just enough of a rise in Willa's tone. "Hmm. I'm trying to decide here if you have something against white ruffles or a thing for sports."

Willa blew out a long sigh and waited a moment before she replied. "No fair, Detective. Interrogations are allowed only while you're on duty."

Now they were getting somewhere. This is what he'd wanted, to touch a nerve, to elicit more than a quick and witty comeback. Joel smiled. "I am on duty. I'm driving."

Willa shifted in her seat. "Is that how it works?"

"Yep. Good cop, bad cop." He pulled to a stop at the next intersection's red light. "Here's the deal. Good cop feeds you lunch. Bad cop won't let you out of the truck until you talk."

She looked at him for a minute, her eyes bright with the captured sunbeams that shone through the broad windshield. The blue sparkled in the light, danced with that energy that lived beneath her skin.

Joel held his breath. That energy was creating his anticipation. An anticipation that was stirring his body and his blood.

"Tell me, Joel." Her smile widened. "Is it the good cop or the bad cop that gets into a staring match with his prisoner and sits though a green light?"

"Damn." Joel spun back around, hit the gas and

made it through the intersection on the tail end of the yellow.

Willa leaned her head into Leigh's and ruffled the baby's curls. Willa's lashes slowly lifted, slowly lowered. If he hadn't known better, he would've thought she was flirting. Thing is, he did know better. He had sisters.

"What a silly uncle you have," Willa crooned to the baby. Leigh giggled and wobbled her head excitedly, up and down, side to side, a circle of angel hair bobbing to no particular beat.

"Not silly." Joel bared his teeth. "Just the better to entertain you with, my dears."

Willa tossed back her head and laughed. "What do you think, Leigh? As long as he keeps his claws and fangs to himself, should we let him entertain us?"

Leigh nodded at Willa's questioning tone and the gurgling giggles began again. Joel rolled his eyes, but kept both hands on the wheel, his focus straight ahead. He needed to consider his strategy. And his strategy required no distractions.

A nice long blacktop highway stretch ahead. That oughta work. He nodded toward it. "Look. No lights. No stop signs. No traffic. Plenty of time for an enlightening discussion of ruffles and cleats."

She twisted her mouth, but didn't say no. He liked it that she hadn't said no. The game was a lot more fun when there was still a chance he might lose. He slowed the truck.

She looked over, lifted a brow. "Been on leave too long, Detective? So long that you're forced to practice interrogation tactics on your neighbor?"

He nodded, lightened his foot on the gas pedal. "Next comes the bamboo under the fingernails."

"And then bread and water once a day?"

"Nah." This one was easy. He'd seen her eat. "Wouldn't want to spoil you."

"All right. All right. I give up. I can't take it any more." She stuck both arms out, wrists up and crossed. "Your driving is torturing me."

"You prefer that I move this along?" He pressed forward five miles per hour, pressed the tension level in the cab up one notch. "I expect to have your full co-operation."

She crossed her heart. "You'll have all the co-operation I can muster."

"You'll tell me about the ruffles?"

She nodded.

"And the cleats?"

She nodded again. Furiously. "Anything and everything. Except about throwing Kristen Hamilton's padded bra into the boy's locker room in tenth grade." She huffed. "C cup my ass."

Oh, yeah, he liked this woman. Liked her a lot. "Tenth grade, huh? Right about the time sixteen-year-old boys are into comparison shopping."

Willa scoffed. "Unlike sixteen-year-old boys to whom size does matter, the problem between the girls is not the size of the cup, but the lies of the wearer."

This was a new one. "Lies?"

"Lies." Arms crossed over her chest, Willa lifted her nose and affected a sixteen-year-old attitude. "Kristen's was padded. Mine wasn't. I proved it. She lost the bet."

Joel had a feeling Willa had been a teenage terror. He clicked his tongue. "Total humiliation."

"She wasn't half as humiliated as I was when I got back from the locker room to find my bra missing." She paused, sank lower in her seat. "And to find it later hanging from the flag pole in the school cafeteria."

It was so damn hard not to laugh. "Bet you got a few looks that day."

"That day and every one after." Willa broke into a smile, the wry twist of her lips one of self-deprecating good humor.

"And that's when you took up soccer, right?" He liked that the memory amused her. "Nothing like a few cleat marks upside the head for payback."

"Actually, I never played soccer. But when I was eleven, I wanted it more than I wanted to breathe."

*More than she wanted to breathe.* The highway rolled by beneath his wheels and Joel wondered what soccer had to do with what Willa'd really wanted. "No cleats then I take it. Just ugly white ruffles."

"They weren't that ugly. They just didn't go well with skateboards and go-karts. Have you ever tried to get tire tread marks out of yellow dotted Swiss?"

A tomboy. Not surprising. "No. But I know how hard it is to get blood out of a white velvet Easter dress. Jen used to pick on me like she was a starving dog and I was the only bone for miles around."

"And one day you picked back?"

"Not picked. Punched. Or tried to. Mine landed short. Hers was right on the nose."

Willa grimaced. "Your nose?"

"Yep. My nose. My blood. Her white dress."

"But you were the boy so the fight was your fault."

"You got it. One size fits all, remember?" He glanced her way then back at the road. "Those frogs and snails and puppy-dog tails chafe after a while."

"Touché."

Joel drifted to the right to give more clearance to a passing car. "Jen and I grew up more as friends than siblings. Which meant when we fought it was fast and furious but short-lived. The battles she waged with Carolyn seemed to last for years."

"I guess that's not unusual for sisters." She shrugged. "I had more boy friends than girl friends."

"It's not too hard to figure out why." He raised a brow at her questioning look. "Not if you made a habit of tossing bras into locker rooms."

She forced a shudder. "They say there are some experiences best lived through but once in a lifetime."

"Like an IRS audit?"

"Oooh." Turning her back to the passenger door, Willa propped her elbow on the top of the car seat that sat between them. "How bad was it?"

Joel wondered if he could belt Leigh's seat on the far right of the cab so Willa could sit closer. "Never had one. Never plan to."

"I don't think they ask permission first." She lifted one of Leigh's curls, let the strands drift back to settle on top of the others. "But you go right ahead and dream."

It was really hard to keep both hands on the

wheel. He wanted to touch Willa's hair the way she was touching Leigh's. He wanted to feel those wild strands spread over his bare chest.

He shook his head. "Been there. Done that. My dream was to be a cop. And I got what I wanted."

"You don't dream about anything else?"

Her voice was soft, her words powerful. Kitten fur with a tiger's bite. Joel felt the impact of both, the first on his senses, the second on his heart.

He laughed off his reaction because it wasn't real. His heart had nothing to do with this. This was all about enjoying Willa with his body and his mind.

It certainly wasn't about dreams he didn't have.

"Hey, whose interrogation is this anyway?" he groused.

"I decided to take over since your concentration seems shot."

"How so?"

"You just passed the turn-off for home."

Joel braked hard, then realized the effort was wasted. Like he was going to stop in the middle of the highway and back up? Criminy. "I'll make you a deal."

"I'm listening."

"I need to make a run to the store if Scout here is going to have anything to eat this week. If you'll push the basket while I hobble down the aisles, I won't mention soccer again."

Willa couldn't keep a straight face. "As long as I don't mention dreams, you mean?"

"Yeah, you see," he said in a Jimmy Cagney aside. "I'd tell you my dreams but—"

"Then you'd have to kill me." Willa interrupted, finishing his sentence.

"Nah. Just kidnap you."

"I see," she said and nodded as if she were thinking it over.

He wanted her to think it over. And over. To consider the possibilities. To come up with ones he hadn't thought of yet. His grip on the steering wheel tightened. "I'd have to keep you restrained, you know."

"I'm sure."

"With handcuffs."

"No doubt you keep several pair on hand."

"Twelve." He couldn't help himself because just the idea was making him sweat.

She squirmed in her seat. "You go through a pair a month, do you?"

"When I'm lucky I go through two."

He arched a brow and glanced her direction. The color in her face was a dead giveaway. He had her where he wanted her. Almost.

She rolled her eyes and glanced at her watch, no-nonsense, black-banded, white-faced. He upped the ante because he wanted to see more of her. There was a lot of time left in the day and the games had just begun.

"Okay. An offer you can't refuse. A charcoal-grilled dinner of your choice."

He watched her mouth twitch and knew she was close. Also knew that what she was fighting, even more than time, was the very thing that assured him he would win this battle.

He knew that by the look in her eyes when she turned her head, when she raised her lashes slowly, when he saw in her eyes a reflection of what he was feeling. The certainty that they were headed toward more than an afternoon spent shopping, an evening spent in front of the grill.

"Well," he prompted, because what had been anticipation was now alive and clawing a hole in his gut. He had to know.

"It depends."

"On?" he prompted again.

"On whether or not you're planning for me to walk a mile for my supper." She nodded toward his gas gauge. "You're runnin' on empty, Wolf Man."

# 5

JOEL BIT OFF a curse. "My schedule's so out of whack I can't even remember to fill up the damn truck."

It was hard for Willa to keep a straight face when she asked, "You schedule your fill-ups?"

"Well…" Joel frowned. "I don't write 'em down on a calendar but, yeah, I gas up about the same time each week. Why?"

"Same time, huh? Same station, too?" Willa's eyebrows went up.

Joel's went further down. "Usually. Why?"

"No reason, really. Just struck me as obsessive-compulsive. Or anal-retentive. Perhaps a combination of the two." He was so incredibly easy to tease. Not to mention a good sport about her doing just that.

"Trust me, Doctor. It's really not that complicated. Just call it a rut and you'll be battin' a thousand." He signaled a turn at the next intersection, pulling into the parking lot of a convenience store that squatted like a small hut in a wooded clearing.

The truck rolled to a stop beneath the pump-island canopy and Joel killed the engine. He draped his arm along the seat and leaned back into his door. "How's this for spur of the moment? Different bat time, different bat station, even."

"Such excitement. Do you think you can stand it?"

"The experience will make a new man out of me." He shot Willa a quick wink and climbed from the truck, sticking his head through the open window to add, "Hold yourself back. If you can."

"I'll do my best," Willa said and grinned.

While Joel worked the nozzle into the tank with one, two, three hollow ringing *whangs*, she turned her attention to Leigh, giving the baby's tummy a quick cootchie-coo. "What a silly uncle you have. Don't you think?"

Leigh flung her head back and forth with exaggerated baby enthusiasm until even Willa grew dizzy. She laughed. "You're right. Silly's hardly the word. Now, sexy's a good one."

Good, yes, but hardly enough, Willa thought, glancing out the rear window at Joel. Sexy was too impersonal, too generic, too conveniently used. It didn't take into consideration all that was Joel.

Sexy had nothing to do with the way he looked at her, those times when he flirted shamelessly with eyes that teased so well, and those other times, when he tentatively tossed out less obvious glances. A few she caught. Others she purposefully chose to let fall in a wily female test of fertile ground.

Sexy had nothing to do with the words he spoke, the come-ons aimed with a shooter's accuracy, the sense of humor that tickled and taunted, the dropped bombs that landed with explosive intention and gave her thoughtful pause.

Sexy had nothing to do with his heart, which was probably more vulnerable than suited a wolf's sense of survival. He'd exposed the roots of his wariness, a telling weakness in an otherwise safe-guarded den where feelings for family huddled deep.

No, sexy was not that all-encompassing, that comprehensive, that...whole. Sexy was too shallow a description for a man like Joel Wolfsley...yet he was the absolute epitome of the word.

*I've lost my mind.* And it was all *his* sexy fault. Willa returned her attention to Leigh who bounced up and back against the seat restraints. Her chatter knob turned to full volume, the baby jabbered and pointed at the store window's bright neon signs.

"You like the scenery, do you? Well, it gets better, girlfriend." Willa tickled Leigh's soft neck and teased her with a kiss dropped on the tip of her nose "Just wait 'til you're my age. By then you'll have a true appreciation of the view."

And what a view it was. Joel had one big hand splayed on the face of the gas pump, the other squeezed the nozzle out of sight. That she couldn't see those fingers didn't matter, because what she could see was telling enough—his biceps and his shoulders and the flex of muscles as he changed the pressure and position of his hold.

And then his face, his focus, changed, too. Where before his gaze had moved from the pump gauge to the storefront to the highway traffic and back, it now narrowed and hardened and remained trained toward the neon lights that had so captivated Leigh's attention.

Even when he shut off the pump, reseated the nozzle and capped his tank, he did it all by rote. His mind was elsewhere, beyond the moment and the task of pumping gas. He opened the driver's-side door then and reached for his cane.

Willa wasn't sure what was wrong though it had to be big to set off the tic in Joel's clenched jaw, the pulsing vein at his temple. Maybe it was his leg? "Why don't you let me go in and pay—"

"No. I'll do it." His tone slapped her back in her seat. The wolf in his eyes kept her there. Now she was worried. "Joel?"

Hackles raised, teeth bared, he raised a hand. "Hush, Willa. Just do what I say."

And now she was frightened. She gripped the padded bar of Leigh's car seat with one hand, braced the other flat on the dash and nodded.

"Good girl. Now, open the glove compartment and slide my gun across the seat. Slowly."

*Gun? Oh, God. His gun.* Her hand slid down the dash. She did what he asked, squeezing upward on the latch. The compartment door bounced on its hinges.

"Slowly, Willa. That's it," he crooned when she pulled out the holstered semi-automatic. "Slide it across the seat like you're passing me a love note in class."

Any other time, she would've smiled. At the mention and reality of the gun, however, she seemed to have lost her sense of humor. Holding her palm flat on the leather-wrapped package, she guided it beneath Leigh's dangling feet until she felt Joel's hand covering hers. He felt like safety and security and, gun or no gun, she trusted him with her life.

"Okay, Baby. I'm going in to pay for the gas." He pulled the pistol from the leather holster, checked the cartridge and tucked it into the small of his back.

"What do you want me to do?" Willa whispered.

Joel's mouth smiled, his eyes did not. "*There's* a question you're gonna have to ask me when I have the time to answer. For now—" nodding more to himself than to her, he jerked his chin back toward the air and water hoses that writhed like a nest of black snakes at the far edge of the store's lot, "—crawl across the seat here and back the truck up to the air pump. I think I've got a low tire."

His tire was about as low as Leigh's sudden high-pitched squeal. Willa shushed the baby and reached for her door handle.

"No," Joel growled. "Don't get out. Just climb over the screamer here and drive."

Willa did as she was told, banging her knee on the steering wheel before sliding her butt into the seat. She looked through the truck's open window at Joel. His gaze shifted between the storefront and…oh, damn…the kid fidgeting near the edge of the building and the bank of pay phones.

"Joel?"

"Hmm," he managed but didn't look her way.

"I have a cell phone in my bag."

Again his eyes darted from point A to point B. This time, though, he took in her face. "Back the truck up, Willa. Swing it around until you're facing the highway…but don't cut the engine. Make sure your door's on the far side and then pop the hood. Whatever you do, don't pull out that phone until the hood is up. Keep it between you and the store. Got it? That's my girl," he added at her nod.

He slapped the truck door as he hobbled away, hobbled more now in fact than he had at any time during the day. Willa swallowed the anxiety that burned from the back of her throat to the center of her chest, then turned over the engine and shifted into reverse.

She eased the truck back, navigating with only half her attention. The other half was caught between Joel and the lookout, which is what the kid had to be. Nervously, he pulled one hand from the deep pocket of his baggy low-riding jeans, scratched at the back of his neck, swiped at his nose and watched Joel's approach, hopping from one foot then the other like a dirty drab flamingo with a nervous twitch.

The closer Joel drew the more the kid hopped until he hopped right up to the glass storefront and rapped his knuckles on the window. Mission accomplished, he backed away, kept backing until he backed into a primered Camaro parked at a cockeyed slant and, judging by the smoky white exhaust, still running.

A robbery. Joel was walking into a robbery. He was armed, yes, but not operating at full capacity. The extent of his limp drove that fact home. Drove home as well the firebrand searing a new taste of danger into Willa's mouth.

She ran her tongue over dry lips, wishing for water to wash away the hot metallic taste, wondering if fear had a smell as sharp and biting. God, what was Joel feeling? Anything like this? Did his heart pound? Did his palms sweat? Or did the wolf inside keep his senses feral and keen?

He'd reached the sidewalk now and, leaning

heavily on his cane, headed toward the lookout with the step, half step of his exaggerated limp. He gestured toward the Camaro with his free hand. The kid nodded, glanced at the car behind him, hopped forward, looked confused. His glances darted from Joel to the car to Joel to the store's glass front door.

Joel had stopped and stood talking to the kid. Willa needed to make her call and make it now, yet she hesitated to leave the truck and Leigh's side. Yes, she needed to trust Joel's instincts. This was his territory, after all. But there was a very female part of her that didn't want to let her Big Bad Wolf out of sight.

Phone in hand, she popped the hood just as the store's front door shot open. Another kid, equally shaggy and baggy pushed through, a paper bag in one hand, a big lug of an antique pistol in the other. Willa didn't even bother to leave her seat. She made her 911 call while the drama around her unfolded.

Joel's cane cut a hard upswing into the wrist of the thief's gun-wielding hand. Gripping his injured wrist and the bulging bag, the kid never saw the downward blow that sent his face scraping the sidewalk and the bag splitting to spill green bills like celebratory confetti.

The lookout saw it all; saw, too, his partner's gun where it had stopped its slide across the pavement at the Camaro's front tire. He took one step then stopped in his tracks. The barrel of Joel's gun directed him down to his knees then flat to his front, his hands laced behind his head.

The store clerk stumbled out then, holding a

wad of brown paper towels to his forehead. At Joel's direction, the man kicked the would-be thief's gun out of reach beneath the car, then cut the Camaro's engine and handed Joel the keys.

Lights flashed at the edge of Willa's vision. Two county cruisers slid into the parking lot. Gravel spewed from beneath the four rear wheels. The cars squealed to a stop at either end of the Camaro, canceling the getaway car's flight plan.

Guns drawn, the sheriffs hit the ground and played out the cops and robbers scene with Hollywood precision. Willa found herself directing their moves; the call for Joel to back away, hands up, gun placed slowly on the ground.

Willa couldn't hear the verbal exchange, but Joel obviously preferred to compromise. He lifted his cast and cane from the bag man's back, tucked his gun barrel in the front of his pants and produced the required ID. The exchange satisfied the sheriffs, one of whom cuffed the shaggy baggy duo while the second questioned both Joel and the store clerk.

Willa wanted nothing more than to get a closer look and listen—unless it was to get the hell out of there. Morbid fascination was a curious thing and kept her where she was. Besides, she'd just had her first glimpse into who the Big Bad Wolf really was. And she was intrigued.

She turned to Leigh whose earlier fidgeting had been quieted by the loud squealing of tires. "Well, Sweetie. What do you think of that? The Big Bad Wolf saved the day."

Leigh chattered and pointed fingers wet from her mouth at Joel.

"Yeah," Willa answered as overwhelming pride

replaced her fear, as respect won out over worry, as admiration grew into more than an appreciation of wide shoulders and big broad hands. Still, she wanted to hit him for scaring the wits out of her. "He's my hero, too."

Her hero shook hands with the arresting officers and, sans limp, headed for the truck. Interesting that, Willa thought. The cunning way he'd taken advantage of an injury that wasn't quite as debilitating as he'd allowed the bad guys to believe.

Interesting too, how he'd first done his best to put her and Leigh out of harm's way. Interesting most of all, was what she felt, watching him draw closer, reading his face for signs of his reaction now that the danger had passed.

She saw none. From all appearances, he hadn't reacted at all. And that she found unbelievable. Joel was a man of deep feelings, so he had to be hiding his response, not wanting her to sense his worry, his fear. Wanting to protect her.

That was it. She was certain. But protect her from what? The crime scene had been contained and she faced no physical danger...

And then the light dawned. He didn't want her to care. Caring led to worry led to fear led to resentment led to anger and the end of relationships.

"Too bad, Wolf Man," she whispered beneath her breath. "I care already."

Joel walked around the front of the truck and shut the hood. His mouth turned up in an offbeat smile when he reached the driver's-side window. "Radiator looks fine."

"I thought it did," she answered, treading this water lightly. "What about the tire?"

He gave a cursory glance to the left rear wheel. "My mistake. Pressure looks good."

"Somehow I thought you'd say that." She backed her way into the passenger seat.

Joel climbed in and slammed the door. Willa waited for him to speak. She had a hundred questions to ask, but first she wanted to hear what he had on his mind.

Apparently nothing. Not even driving, she decided when he made no move to put the truck in gear.

"Joel?"

"Hmm?"

"When you were at the Police Academy..." He glanced her way. "...Did you take a course in cane safety?"

He blinked hard for a minute and then he grinned his devil's grin. "Cane Safety 101. One of those courses it never hurts to have under your belt. Amazing how it all comes back to you."

"You looked like an old pro."

"I did, didn't I?" he said, but then his grin slowly faded. "We'll talk later, Willa. Right now I'd like to get home." And then he put the truck into reverse. Not drive, which would take them out to the highway, but reverse, and swung around to head for the store.

The teens had since been relegated to the back seats of the cruisers. The paramedics, who had arrived on the heels of Joel's return to the truck, were finishing up with the store clerk. Willa gathered by the pantomime he'd performed that the injury to his forehead had come from the butt end of the gun.

Everything seemed to be under control, so what were they doing here? Willa nodded toward the sheriffs. "Do you need to stay until they're finished?"

Joel shook his head. "They have my name and number. They'll get in touch when they need to."

"Then what are we doing here?"

There was that grin again. "Now, Willa, what kind of example would I be if I drove off without paying for my gas?"

And leaving her with Leigh once again to wait, he hopped down from the truck.

JOEL WONDERED what it felt like to have a heart attack, because there was something strange going on in his chest. He guessed he could've let the medics take a listen, but then he'd have felt like a fool when they told him he was sweating through the end of an adrenaline rush.

He knew that. He'd experienced it once or twice and medicated the feeling with a stiff drink. But those times he'd been on the job, not on his own time. And the fear had been for innocent bystanders, his fellow officers and, okay, a bit for himself. But it hadn't been for his niece and his next-door neighbor—two very important females in his life.

Pulling out of the parking lot, he eased back into the light highway traffic, leaving the convenience store to be swallowed up by the surrounding tall pines and live oaks. Thankful that both of his passengers, for the moment at least, seemed to accept his silence, he kept his eyes on the road and his mouth shut. Because he sure wasn't in any mood to talk.

This morning and through lunch, with Willa and the baby, he'd actually, stupidly entertained a fleeting notion of having a family of his own. Not an idea he'd weighed seriously, of course. Just one he'd tried on for size. A bad fit, the incident at the store proved once and for all.

He'd be a lot better off sticking with the tried and true, going with what he knew worked for him. He wasn't going to risk losing something that it would kill him to lose. He'd been faced with threats of revenge, promises of retribution.

But never before had he experienced the type of test he'd faced today, being off-duty, in the wrong place at the wrong time and having to react as he had because Detective Joel "the Big Bad Wolf" Wolfsley, could do no less.

Never, ever did he want to face that situation again. Even now, a claw of fear had yet to let go of his gut. Instead it took hold and dug deep. He tried to shake it. Decided it might be best if he didn't.

It wouldn't be a bad thing to have it around as a reminder of today. Especially when he got it in his head to question decisions he'd resolutely lived with now for years.

Because if he'd been this scared over Willa, how would he feel about a woman he loved?

WILLA HAD YET to decide if the fish had been a good idea or a bad one. The upside was that the meal had been one of the best—and one of the only— she'd had in a while. She got like that, though. Busy to the point that she neglected to eat. Or at least neglected to eat a rounded diet.

She subsisted instead on fresh fruits and vegetables from the farmers' market. More often than not she ate them raw and on the run, along with the home-baked bread Mrs. Craig brought over once a week. So, in that regard—iodine and iron and all that—the fish had been a good idea.

Joel hadn't exaggerated his skill with a grill and a handful of charcoal briquettes. She loved a man who could cook. And Joel had been such a good sport. He'd skewered the chunks of peppers, tomatoes and zucchini she'd chopped and then popped the kabobs on the fire, roasting the vegetables alongside the foil-wrapped fillets cooking in seasoned butter.

The fish had melted on her tongue. The vegetables had plumped up with sweet juices and burst with kaleidoscopic flavor in her mouth. She'd savored each and every bite, and had eaten way too much. In fact, Willa thought, taping a clean diaper around the squirming baby's chubby tummy, she felt a lot like Leigh looked.

"What do you think, Sweetie?" she asked, tickling the soft skin above the diaper before asking her next question, her real question—a question that wasn't about what they'd eaten at all but about the deeper layers of the day. "Was the fish a good idea?"

Leigh answered with a fuss, doing her best to scramble down from the couch. Willa chuckled. Her need for a little female bonding would just have to wait. At the moment, the baby's one-track mind was in play mode. And there was no need to clean her up now only to have to do it again later, especially since clothing was still a problem.

The grocery shopping trip had turned into a very

long afternoon. Between fixings for the meal and baby supplies for the week—not to mention the holdup—they'd made more stops than originally planned. And though he'd never admit it, Willa knew the going, going, going had tired Joel.

She'd studied his face throughout the day and noticed the imperceptible changes. The grooves at the corners of his mouth had deepened into slashes of exhaustion. And the sunburst of laugh lines fanning out from his eyes had dug deep as if he'd had to pry loose the crow.

She'd noticed it especially after they'd stopped for gas and stayed to uphold the law. That couldn't have been easy on Joel. He was already working with a handicap—though the truth of that statement wouldn't have been easy to prove. The way he'd moved she could've believed both the cane and cast to be props.

But the danger had been real enough and it hadn't taken the gun to convince her. No, the truth had come later, in Joel's face as he drove, the way his eyes seemed glassy, though she knew they were singularly focused because he missed every pit in the asphalted road.

He'd been deep in thought and silent, yet by the time he'd next stopped the truck he seemed to have come to a decision. Or at least an acceptance that he'd done the right thing and done it well.

It couldn't have been easy for him, knowing his niece had been as close to the danger as Willa had been. That factor had to have tipped the scales toward the plan of action he judged best, one he could live with both as an uncle and an officer of the law.

He hadn't acted rashly, that Willa knew. Both the care he'd taken to see to her safety and Leigh's and the vulnerable exposure he'd willingly walked into, had increased her admiration for Joel as a man. Yet the outcome had taken its toll.

At their last stop, the fish market, the foot of his cane caught a snag in the doorway's metal flashing. He'd broken his fall against the nearest display case; the flat of his hand smacking the glass front and jarring a particularly large flounder from his lettuce bed.

Even after leaving the shop with that same fish wrapped in white paper and tucked beneath his arm, Joel still refused to admit his recovering body had reached its limit. Willa had taken charge then and insisted they get Leigh home. She hadn't offered a reason and Joel hadn't asked.

So, they'd never made it by Jennifer's house to pick up more clothes and check on Shadow. First thing in the morning, Joel had said, looking more than a little relieved as he'd moved Leigh's Exersaucer from the living room to the deck. He'd stopped Willa then, just as she'd headed for home to check on the dogs before dinner.

His hold had been firm on her upper arm, the look in his eyes deep and intense as he'd made sure she understood he was including her in tomorrow's plans. And that as far as he was concerned, this particular day was not even close to being over.

It had been hard to concentrate on what needed to be done at the kennels after that. But she'd gotten her strength training for the day with Tic Toc's tug-o'-war toy plus an aerobic workout with Loverboy and his Frisbee, then scratched Mickey's ears until the dog was a spineless five pounds in her hands. The Dalmatian pup remained curled in a trembling ball and Willa talked softly until he'd drifted off to sleep.

Gordy had accompanied Willa back to Joel's then, and while the adults had cooked, he'd made it his duty to shepherd the baby and her things. Leigh had adored the canine attention. Which is why she was so impatient to get off her uncle's sofa and back outside to the dog.

Willa lifted the baby from the leather cushions and headed toward the kitchen door, doing her best not to snoop as she moved from the one room to the other. Yes, she and Joel had become amazingly well acquainted in an incredibly short span of time. But that didn't give her the right to wonder why there was an unmailed envelope and nothing else on his mantel. Why he had no throw rugs on his hardwood floor, no pictures on his walls. Why the only pieces of furniture in the living room were the sofa and a big-screen TV. She wondered, regardless, and wanted the right to do just that, the right to ask and have him answer.

Which is why the fish had been a bad idea.

More than once the three of them had been mistaken for a family. A young couple with a child. They'd had way too much fun shopping this afternoon, laughing and teasing and shamelessly flirting. At least until Joel had taken his tumble in the fish market. The drive home, after that, had been subdued.

Willa had taken the assumptions in stride, savored them probably more than she should have, but, hey, a girl was entitled to dream. Joel had been the one quick to set everyone straight, the waitress and cashier at the diner, the fisherman who'd sold them the flounder in the market, the various sales clerks who'd rung them out from the grocery to the baby specialty store.

Joel might deny he was a family man, or at least husband and father material, but his quick denials were doing more to convince Willa otherwise. Not that what she believed mattered. Just that Joel would one day need to learn this for himself. She suspected that as with most men, all it would take would be the right woman. Funny how men hated admitting that truth.

A part of her thought she would like very much to get to know the Wolf Man better. Her practical side was, well, more practical. It would hardly be fair to work on a permanent relationship when neither of them met the other's idea of a partner.

But in the meantime the attraction between them had amazing possibilities. She worked long, hard hours to make sure her business thrived. Loneliness lurked on the edges of her life but it wasn't a constant nag. Certainly not an enemy. She was happy, and she was sure Joel was the same. That didn't mean they couldn't or shouldn't enjoy one another's company.

"Friends and lovers" was not an unheard-of concept, and the more she thought, the more she was certain she and Joel could have a very good time for as long as the fun lasted.

"Here we are," she said, stepping out of the kitchen. Joel was sprawled in a lounger on the redwood deck built along the back of the house.

They'd finished eating a half hour ago, yet Willa felt a wave of heat when she walked past the grill to put a momentarily content Leigh into her saucer seat.

"Dinner was wonderful." Willa settled back into the cedar lounger next to Joel's. Legs crossed at the ankle, arms braced on the rests, she released a purr of contentment. "I like to cook, but I seem never to have time for anything more elaborate than a pot of soup."

"It *was* good, wasn't it?" He turned his head and blinked sleepily. "And thanks for the suggestion. The fish was a great idea."

She didn't contradict him, even though she'd already worked through that argument in her mind, albeit unsatisfactorily. "Just don't get too comfortable over there. Your little one is about ready for a bath and bedtime."

Joel stretched his arms high overhead, arching his back like a big cat. She half expected a deep rumbling roar. She half expected him to scoot to the right, settle back and pat the empty space at his side, making room for her to join him. He didn't and she admitted to an unexpected disappointment.

"I think your warning's about ten minutes too late." He rubbed at his eyes, passed his hand down his face and chuckled. "I'm already too comfortable."

She was sure that he was. And that her head would fit nicely against his shoulder. "So I see."

"Yep. Fat and happy and ready to curl up and sleep for a day or two."

"Too much food'll do that to you."

"So will too much beer, too much time in the weight room, too much...sun." His mouth twitched as he fought a grin. He thought she'd thought he was going to say sex.

Typical man. Of course, she *had* thought he was going to say sex. But she wasn't about to admit it. "Hmm. The evils of excess."

"No, the pleasure of enjoying a good thing. Being able to sleep like a baby is one of the best."

She wanted to watch him sleep. She wanted to sleep next to him, to snuggle into his side, to feel his warmth, to breathe deeply of his skin. He was a protector, an honorable man. He took care of his own and did it well.

He had what she didn't. The love of a family.

This particular family was growing on her rapidly, adding another layer to the comforts she held close. She glanced from Joel to Leigh whose head was nodding, whose tiny fists were rubbing tiny eyes.

Willa smiled and nodded towards Leigh. "You mean the ability to sleep anytime and anywhere? That trait seems to run in your family."

"Ah, the munchkin. I'd better get her tucked in for the night." Joel swung around and sat sideways on the lounger, his casted foot bumping up against Willa's seat. He braced one palm on the arm of the chair, the other on his good thigh and pushed to his feet.

And then he frowned. The cane rested on the deck just behind his heel. He realized where it was just as Willa did. She dipped forward from her chair as Joel came down.

His face was oh so close. She could smell the

smoke of the evening on his clothes, detect the subtler scents of soap and after shave. Cupping his cheek with her palm before he'd fully straightened seemed the thing to do.

So she did.

# 6

HIS END-OF-THE-DAY BEARD was coarse, his jaw strong and set. His eyes were softly green, his lashes thick, and full and beautifully masculine.

Willa thought of cattails along a marsh. The wings of a mallard colored by nature's palette. Hunting dogs and horses and a race across the ground.

But then she quit thinking because he smiled. The evening brightened and Joel's face became the sun. Willa absorbed the warmth through her pores and shivered.

The response was part anticipation, part exquisite sensation of being held captive, and she delighted in both.

Slowly, Joel's fingers came up to wrap around hers then twine with hers. He sank back to his chair and captured her knees between his cast and his leg. He explored her nails, blunt and short as her work required, and her skin, not as soft as she wished or as smooth as that of a woman who didn't handle animals for a living.

But none of her flaws seemed to matter to Joel. His smile was as much a surrender as a measure of his mood and frame of mind. "I *am* going to need help, you know. I can't even get out of a chair under my own steam."

"I think you're suffering from too much fish, not a lack of steam." Her voice sounded husky in her ears, felt heavy as it rolled up from the deep of her throat.

"I think you're right." He took each of her fingers one by one and stroked from the base to the tip. "Steam isn't the problem."

She took a deep breath, started to take back her hand, but left it in his because she was learning the beauty of waiting, of letting satisfaction take its time. "No, Joel. You're wrong."

"How so?"

She met his beguiling gaze. "Steam *is* the problem here."

He pressed the whole of her hand between both of his. "Is this a problem?"

"You holding my hand?" Though what he was doing to her hand was closer to making love. "Or what's been happening between us today that neither of us is talking about?"

He gave a one-shouldered, casual shrug and glanced across the deck at Leigh who was totally absorbed with Gordy. "We're talking about it now."

"Are we? Sounds to me like we're talking around it." But the subject was out in the open and she was glad. Innuendoes and evasions had been the order of the day. Silly when they were both adults.

And when the attraction each felt for the other might not have been voiced but had most definitely been heard. Heard in the rush of blood like water over rock. In the beat of a heart like a pounding rain. In thoughts building like rapids roaring.

"That's the beauty of the dance, Willa." Joel closed his eyes slowly, took a deep breath and opened them again. "You gotta have the music before you take the first step."

His fingers waltzed along the back of her hand. "Do you hear it?"

What she heard was Joel. Oh, how she heard Joel. With her eyes, with her heart, with her busy, busy analytical mind. With her skin.

His touch was music, masterfully played. One finger then the next plucked the strings of her palm. His thumb added another layer to the song, pressing down hard with a deep bass resonance that she felt in the bones of her wrist.

It was a song of seduction, a song of man to woman. A melody sweet and hypnotic that delivered her to the verge of an emotion far beyond tears. Her body could do nothing but follow the rhythm he set, accompany him through the first movement, then the next.

The thought was sobering, that a man she knew in a most casual way had the potential to be her Pied Piper. But the very thought that left her unsettled, soothed her at the same time. For it was Joel's touch she wanted, no other man's.

Pushing up the cuff of her flannel, he moved to her wrist, holding the back of her hand in his palm. The circles he thumbed on her forearm scraped with a delicious tickle and Willa shivered.

"I like that you're listening, Willa. I want you to hear. This sound…" he paused, drawing the circles back toward her wrist, then tracing the design further up her arm "…this is the sound of foreplay."

She whimpered. Her body quickened. She

wanted Joel to touch her in intimate places, to make her body sing. To relieve the tension that was humming like a live wire just beneath her skin.

Her eyes were closed when he shifted on his seat and leaned forward. The air around her heated with the warmth of his body, the temperature of her own.

She sensed Joel's hands near her throat, knew she'd sensed correctly when the placket of her unbuttoned flannel skated over her ribbed white tank, slid down to her elbows where it bound her arms at her sides.

When the night breeze passed in a whisper, gooseflesh pebbled her skin. And when she felt Joel's mouth in the barest touch, felt him hum low in his throat, heard the call of his music, the whole of her body burst into song.

Joel feathered kisses along her collarbone. Her breasts swelled, her nipples drew taut and by Joel's sharp intake of breath she knew he was visually aware of the effect of his touch.

His hair brushed her jaw as his mouth moved into the hollow of her throat. His tongue darted out to tickle and tease and leave wet circles on her skin.

It wasn't enough and it was too much and if she didn't get her hands on him soon she was going to come apart.

Her fingers spread in her lap, her hands reached toward him, unable to move for the bonds at her elbows—bonds from which he refused to release her when she made a negligible move against his hold.

"No. Not yet," he said, his words warm where his breath brushed her neck. His fists, where they held her shirt, knuckled up beneath her breasts, pressing into the pliant undersides. "The dance, remember?"

She nodded. Imperceptibly. That was all she could do with his hands where they were. Finally where they were. "Does this dance have steps?"

"Those we make up as we go along," he answered with a Big Bad Wolf grin.

His steps, she thought to herself, and said, "I see," though she didn't see at all because her eyes were closed while she waited for him to take a bite. "This step would be called, 'The Better To Eat You With, My Dear'?"

"My pleasure."

He moved up and caught her whispered words with his mouth. His lips touched hers. Briefly. Barely. Only long enough for her to feel the lightest texture of the mouth she'd had her eyes on all day.

A wolf with the touch of a lamb, soft and gentle. She'd expected no less though she'd had no expectations. She remained unmoving while he drew on her lower lip. He tasted of the night air and smelled of the same, woodsy and darkly seductive.

She wanted more, a deeper sampling of his flavor. She wanted to tangle her tongue with his, to feel the edges of his teeth, to press her lips hard beneath his and open her mouth.

"Joel," she whispered, her tongue flicking out to savor his dampness on her lower lip.

"Willa," he answered, nipping at her upper lip now. His fists full of flannel pressed upward until the backs of his fingers grazed nipples taut and tender.

Desire blossomed wet and wild between her legs and this was only a kiss. A kiss that bordered on benign for all its lack of passion, yet as arousing as any she'd ever shared with a man.

This was Joel's music, Joel's song, and Willa listened with skin that prickled from the feel of his beard and his breath. Listened with her tasting, teasing mouth.

Listened with a heart that had been hopeful for a very long time, anticipating a melody that would fill the longing she had for a life partner.

Slowly, Willa stiffened, pulled out of the kiss by the intrusive thought…and something more. That wasn't what this was about. This was about the moment and nothing beyond.

Together, she and Joel had the potential for great fun. They'd proved that today. And if the past eight hours had been stolen from time, she'd gladly look back and remember the diner, the fish market, the baby and this kiss.

But there could be nothing permanent between them, now or in the future. She opened her eyes as Joel moved away.

"I think he's trying to get your attention."

"What?" Still dazed and wary, Willa heard again what had nipped at her daydream. Gordy's bark. One sharp yap, insistent yet patient. She glanced over her shoulder. The dog sat at the front of Leigh's saucer seat, looking at Willa, at the baby and back again.

"Oh, Sweetie," Willa said and left her chair as she should've done hours—was it hours?—ago. She crossed the deck to where Leigh sat in her seat, her hand reaching across the tray toward the dog, her head lolled to one side, her tiny lips parted in slumber.

Willa lifted the baby who opened drowsy eyes and frowned. Leigh fussed her displeasure at being disturbed and guilt drove away Willa's lingering arousal. Some help she was. Leigh needed a change not to mention a real bath and a bottle. And here Willa was dancing.

"Hey, Scout." Joel spoke near Willa's ear. He reached across her shoulder to smooth the baby's hair. "You about ready to turn in?"

Leigh reached for her uncle then and Willa surrendered the tiny package. Once the baby was safely tucked against her uncle's shoulder, Willa jammed her hands in the back pockets of her jeans and took a step back and away.

"Cuttin' out on me?" Joel asked, one brow lifted.

"It's late." She couldn't explain her withdrawal except to think of it as a safety net. These two would manage fine without her. And if she stayed…well…she'd be stepping off into dangerous territory. "I've got that one pup I really need to see to."

Joel shook his head. "Willa. You don't have to explain."

"Yes. I do. I offered help. You accepted. And now…" She let the sentence drift, took another step back.

"Call it an underhanded attempt to get you where I want you." When she frowned, he added, "A guy thing. Don't worry about trying to figure it out."

"I'll stay. If you really want me to, I'll stay."

"I want you to stay. But not to help me with Scout here. She and I did fine last night with the bath and bedtime routine." He gently bounced the dozing baby. "If you stay, it'll be for me. And I don't think you're quite ready for that.

He was right. As much as she was, she wasn't. "Thank you."

"For what?" he asked, his mouth quirked upward.

"For being a nice man."

His laugh was belly deep and full of the Big Bad Wolf. "You'd better go, Willa. Before I disprove your theory."

Rising up on tiptoes, she brushed her lips over his. "I'm more afraid that you'll prove it. I have a feeling you can be nice in ways I haven't thought of."

"You've thought of a lot, have you?"

"The better to keep secret from you," she said then turned and whistled for Gordy. She was down the steps and halfway through their shared hedge when Joel's back light went off.

Moonlight bathed the yard. And the low howl that reached her ears was an eerily fitting cry.

WILLA SLEPT WELL, but not long. She wasn't sure if it was the whimper of the Dalmatian pup that woke her or the memory of Joel's seductive call.

She knew why he'd done it, why he'd howled into the dark of the night. The sound had been one of frustration, a letting-off of built-up steam. She understood the feeling.

Although the evening had held the warmth of the early spring day, she'd been shivering when she reached her back door, wondering what she'd walked away from, what would have happened had she stayed behind.

Instead of a long low howl at the moon, she'd had to make do with a long relaxing bubble bath. The relaxing part hadn't been easy to get to. By the time she had, the hour had been late and she had been pruned.

She'd wanted to be ready this morning when Joel called, so she'd set her alarm accordingly and allowed herself enough time to see to the dogs. She hadn't even slept as long as she'd planned because that lone mournful cry had pulled her from sleep. Once fully awake, she knew that what she'd heard had been the Dalmatian. Joel's song was all in her mind.

The pup had been hungry enough to venture from the corner of the pen where he'd cowered since yesterday morning. He'd eaten well enough to suit Willa and the light in his eyes reassured her that his recovery wouldn't be forever in coming. After a little extra attention and coddling, she moved on.

Her other boarders, stuck spending spring break in a kennel, had patiently waited their turns—then demanded 100 percent of her energy and attention. Tic Toc had been especially eager to stretch his legs and Willa could hardly say no to a paying customer.

So, as anxious as she was to start her day with Joel—and why *was* she so anxious?—she first saw to the animals' needs. After a short game of fetch with Loverboy and an extra five minutes of scratching Mickey's ears, she'd changed into running shoes and sweats and done her good doggy deed for the day. Tic Toc had thanked her with a wide slobbery smile.

By the time she heard Joel's back door open and close, heard his uneven step on the stairs leading down from his deck, heard him open the door to his truck, she'd already showered, dressed for the third time that morning and was ready for the day.

Living out as far as they did, hearing those sounds from Joel's place had been easy—even if she wasn't listening. Which, admittedly, she was. But she knew he'd wanted to get an early start. And she didn't want to keep him waiting.

Willa brushed off the knees of her jeans, then the seat, wished she had a more casual, less roughneck wardrobe, came to her senses and grabbed up the chambray shirt she'd left on the workbench in the kennel area.

After pulling the long-sleeved cover-up over her goldenrod tank top, she told Gordy to stay and cut through the hedge for Joel's. She found him checking the security of the baby seat. A mug of coffee steamed from the ledge of the truck bed.

"Good morning," she said, directing the words over his shoulder.

He pulled the last strap tight and glanced over his shoulder before backing out of the cab. "You're up and about early."

His smile was sleepy, as were his eyes, and Willa felt her heart flip then flop. "It's not so early. Not when I have a kennel full of children who want to play the minute the sun's up."

A guilty flush crept up Joel's neck. "Well, Scout and I decided to sleep in for a while. We spent a late night watching Lethal Weapon."

"The first one?"

"And the second. I thought about the third, but

it was already past one. And by then the munch-kin'd had her fill of Mel." Grinning, he reached for his coffee.

And while he sipped, Willa studied. His jeans were well-worn as was his single brown leather cowboy boot with its scuffed toe and sloped heel. His belt buckle was silver, inlaid with nuggets of turquoise. And his T-shirt—of course a T-shirt—was obviously new and dark, dark black.

"You want a cup?"

"What?" Willa shook off what she could of her daze. Why did he look so good this morning? He was the same man who'd been her neighbor for a year, the same man who waved at her across their shared hedge, who said hello and asked about her day when they met at the mailbox.

The same man who'd kissed her tenderly on his deck last night.

He lifted his mug. "Coffee? Caffeine?" He frowned. "You sure you're awake, Willa? You're looking a little glassy-eyed."

She was surprised her eyes were even open be-cause she was sure she'd just been dreaming, re-membering that kiss. She touched her lower lip, which trembled. "Sure. Coffee sounds great."

Joel slammed the truck door, placed his free hand in the small of her back and guided her to-ward the deck. "I've got sugar, but I'm not sure about milk." He chuckled. "Unless you want to give Scout's formula a shot."

"Funny. And just sugar is fine." She walked up the stairs ahead of him, turned to wait and realized he was leaning heavily on the railing as he made his way up. "What happened to your cane?"

He shook his head, stepped onto the deck, limped toward her. "Nothing. It's in the house. I thought after falling on my face in the fish market yesterday I'd give it a rest."

"Makes sense. This way when you fall on your face you can fall on your face." *Men*.

"Yeah, well. I'm getting tired of relying on the damn thing," he said, opening the back door. "It's not like I don't have two legs."

Like she'd said, *men*. Willa entered the kitchen, inhaled the fresh-brewed coffee and headed for the pot. She pulled a mug down from the cupboard above and poured.

"Bein' up at the crack of dawn, I guess you've eaten breakfast?"

Eyes closed as she sipped, Willa nodded. Then she glanced at Joel whose cup was empty, whose eyes were slowly waking and whose stomach loudly growled. She grinned. "I had a zucchini bran muffin and an apple."

"So you *haven't* eaten." Joel's arched brow made a powerful argument in his favor.

Of course, to the Big Bad Wolf, fruit and fiber did not a breakfast make. "I ate. But since then I've played fetch and Florence Nightingale. I could eat again."

"Good, because I haven't eaten a thing since last night." Joel's early-morning sleepy grin slowly took over his face and Willa felt her hold on her mug and her composure begin to slip.

"So? What's on the menu?" She set the mug on the counter, pulled open the fridge, peered inside then raised a questioning brow. "Beef and beer?"

"Bachelor grub. I warned you."

"And after all that shopping we did yesterday."

"We bought diapers and formula and fish," Joel said, moving into Willa's space to refill his coffee, brushing up against her—subtly—when he reached for the pot.

Knowing she wouldn't find anything but the breathing room and the distraction she desperately needed, Willa leaned down to peer in the crisper drawers. Seemed she was wrong. "Aha. Bacon. Unopened. Unexpired. I think we're in business."

"We would be. If I had eggs."

"As luck would have it, I *do* have eggs." She glanced back over her shoulder and up into his eyes. It was hard to think clearly when he looked at her that way, like he wanted more than bacon and eggs for breakfast. "Give me five minutes?"

"I have coffee. I should be able to stave off starvation until you get back." A demanding baby cried from the living room and Joel brought his mug up in salute. "Or until the munchkin wakes."

Willa left the bacon on the center shelf and closed the fridge. "Do you want me to see to her?"

Joel shook his head, placed his mug in the sink. "I'd rather you see to my eggs. If that's not too caveman for you."

"I think I can do caveman," Willa said and gave her best grunt.

Joel laughed. "I knew I liked you, Willa Darling. Now, go, woman. Get eggs. Cook breakfast. Feed man."

And she went, rolling her eyes as she did so, figuring once in a while a little caveman never hurt anyone.

JOEL WAS GETTING way too used to having Willa around—and she'd only been around for one day. This was not a good thing. He told himself that his enjoyment of her company had to do with the help she'd given him with Leigh. This was a lie.

Because right now Willa wasn't helping with the munchkin at all. She had her back to him, in fact, and he'd never enjoyed her company more.

Scout sat on his knee as he fed her cereal and bananas. After taking one look at the day-old white dress, he'd tied a dish towel around the baby's neck and over her pajamas, figuring at her age she could get away with staying in her night clothes all day.

And now that Willa was here and ready, they could pick up the rest of the things they needed from Jen's. Not that he was going to rush Willa with breakfast. It was nice watching a woman cook and he wasn't through with his very tame foray into voyeurism.

Not too many women had cooked in this kitchen. His mother and Jen had both pulled KP when he'd come home from the hospital. And he seemed to remember the wife of a buddy or two making use of the stove top. But none of those women had been worth watching the way Willa was worth watching.

He liked the way she wore her clothes. Her wardrobe was casual and practical, plain but not plain at all. That made no sense, he knew, but the way she pulled the simple pieces together gave the impression of high fashion. Or maybe it was just the way she moved, lithely, economically yet as elegantly as any woman who made her living on a runway.

What struck him the most, however, was how Willa could make the switch from outdoors to indoors without so much as a blink. She cracked eggs with one hand, knew by a sniff of the air when to turn the bacon, had rolled and cut biscuits to fit a man's appetite. None of those skills was peculiar to Willa or particularly difficult.

But he didn't know another woman who could whip through the full breakfast routine and calm forty pounds of frightened teeth and claws with the same ease. He'd yet to see her tackle a task with anything but confidence.

He wondered what she'd be like in bed.

He wondered how long it would be before he found out. Because he would find out. He knew that—had known that since he'd drunk coffee across the table from her twenty-four hours ago.

Willa Grace Darling said more with her eyes than she did with words. Eyes were Joel's specialty, a fact of life he wasn't quite ready to let her in on. Right now, he wanted to keep the upper hand.

That is, if he'd ever had it.

# 7

JENNIFER AND ROB COLLINS lived a good hour's drive from the wooded area both Willa and Joel called home. The development northeast of Houston was known as The Livable Forest, a neighborhood with tremendous appeal to young upwardly mobile families.

Willa preferred her corner of the world—not that she didn't appreciate the aesthetic beauty of the planned community and Jennifer's warmly welcoming home in particular. The Collinses' place, for all its trendy façade, had the cozy ambiance of a mountain lodge done in deep greens and cranberry accents.

But Willa was too used to her less-structured way of life to envy what she admittedly admired. She and Joel seemed to have that in common, she mused, following him through the winding hallways of the vast ground floor and listening to his grumbled complaints about home builders and master plans.

He stopped in the doorway to Leigh's nursery and glanced around the room of the bright reds and purples. "Two adults and a ten-month-old in a house the size of Idaho. I'd question my sister's sanity if I didn't know this place was a drop in the bucket of what she and Rob can afford."

Willa barely held her grin. "And it's none of your business anyway, right?"

"Right." He shot her a teasing glare then stepped inside and glanced around the room, hands braced at his lean waist as his gaze roamed. "Besides, Rob's sanity is even more suspect. Letting Jen loose with a paintbrush in here. Where was the man's head?"

Willa moved past Joel to put a squirming Leigh on the floor of familiar territory. She took off on two wobbly feet, heading for a stack of soft alphabet blocks, fairly diving into the center of the colorful cotton plush pile.

"I thought you approved of the color choices." She watched Joel watch Leigh, feeling more than a small jolt in the region of her heart at the tender expression that reached up to crinkle the corners of his eyes. "Something about child development and primary colors and a psychological connection?"

He shook his head, smiling as his niece pointed up at him and gurgled. "I'm afraid I'm gonna have to jump on Rob's bandwagon here. This room has sixties' peace rally written all over it."

"It's not that bad." Willa took in the purple and red counterpane, crib bumpers, ruffle and curtains, the yellow and green accents on lamp shades and the splashy combination of the same colors in broad brush strokes on white walls. "Leigh certainly doesn't mind."

The baby was face down in the heap of cushy toys, now, rubbing her cheeks against the material and cooing quietly to herself. Her knees were tucked to her tummy, her hair lay in silky disarray. Her eyes were closed and her mouth was working, making sweet baby bubbling noises through a sweet baby smile.

Willa felt a maternal tug pull at her belly and breast. Moments such as these were rare, and treasured more for being so, treasured for the pure innocence that was found in chubby tummies and angel cheeks, thickly diapered skyward rumps and tiny fingers nursed by tiny mouths.

They were treasured for the awareness that she would have to take these moments as they came, few and far between, enjoying the precious quiet times with babies who would never be her own.

If she envied Jennifer Collins anything, it was that she would see her child grow and experience the wondrous changes brought by each passing year. Willa had her own wellspring of blessings, but still she wished she might have known the same.

A deep breath and she looked up to find Joel watching her watch Leigh. His gaze was more than a casual acknowledgment of her interest, nearly an involved attentiveness to what she was feeling—and why. She chalked it up to curiosity and let it be.

At least she thought she had. Until she heard the sound of her voice and found herself answering the questions he'd silently, wordlessly asked.

"I had an accident. When I was ten." She hugged her arms beneath her breasts and followed the baby's antics. "A silly slip of footing while climbing a fence. The same fence I'd scrambled over dozens of times. I guess I was a little too sure of myself, you know?"

She gave a small laugh. Sure of herself barely

covered the young hoyden she'd been. "I have a couple of nice scars to show for that Humpty Dumpty spill, but the worst of the damage was internal. The doctor who put me back together again said my chances for having children couldn't be any worse."

Joel screwed his eyes closed, opened them slowly. Sorrowfully. "What does the doctor say now?"

"Not much of anything new," she answered, her voice soft in the silence of the loud room.

"I'm sorry—"

She cut him off with a shake of her head. If she wanted anything from Joel, it certainly wasn't pity. "Don't be. Seriously. It happened a long time ago."

He rubbed a hand over the back of his neck, watching as Leigh settled into the comfortable nest she'd burrowed for herself. He nodded toward the baby. "I've seen you with Scout, you know."

"Please don't tell me I'd make a good mother." She'd never worked out in her mind why that particular platitude should make her feel better. "And, yes. Before you say anything I know adoption's an option."

He nodded, seemed to think. "So's step-parenting."

She shrugged. "Sure. If it happens."

"And if it doesn't?"

"Then it doesn't. It's not like I'm about to let the issue of children make or break a relationship," she added under her breath.

It seemed a long minute later when Joel said, "That's happened to you, hasn't it?"

She stuffed her hands in her front pockets, unsure how far to take what was personal and really not relevant to what might or might not happen between her and Joel.

"Once or twice, yeah," she settled on saying. "Nice guys who've said they don't mind not having children. At least until it comes down to the wire and they're hit with the epiphany that children are exactly what they want."

"What do *you* want?" he asked, his voice searching and sympathetic, but still wary.

Enough of the depressing stuff. She tilted her head to one side, cast him a glance from beneath her lashes. "In a relationship? Or in a good time?"

Joel snorted. "1-900-Big-Boys will get you a good time. I figure you're looking for more than that."

"Eventually, sure. But I don't plan to rush true love or happily ever after. And in the meantime I'd like more company than my own."

"You shouldn't have a hard time finding... company." Joel's voice was low. The once-over he gave her spoke volumes.

"Because I'm tall and leggy and blond?" She knew she'd interpreted his comment correctly by the appreciative male look that darkened his eyes—a look that sparked a purely female thrill, raising the tiny hairs on her spine. "You're right. I don't. Or at least I didn't."

He raised a brow. "You've stopped looking?"

"Just taking a break. The tall, blond, leggy thing seems to be a chaff magnet." She walked the length of Leigh's crib, ran a finger down the side railing. "I got tired of weeding through the chaff."

"So, what do you do now? For...company?"

Interesting the way they'd chosen to talk around

the subject of sex. She turned to face him. "I haven't had *company* for a very long time. I miss that. But, because I'm a woman...well, it gets complicated."

"You mean the perception that women don't? When women really do?" Joel asked, his smile too knowing for Willa's state of mind.

"Why is that so hard to understand? I'm not deaf to the buzz of the birds and bees." She fought a grin and lost. "I just have a different set of...antennae than a man."

"And a very nice set of antennae you have there, too," Joel replied in a perfectly awful Groucho Marx, tamping the ash from an air cigar.

Her grin widened. He really did draw out her inner vamp. And, well, why not. No need to be coy about what she wanted. "The better with which to pick up your signals, my dear."

Eyebrows paused in midwiggle, Joel cupped a hand to one ear, stepped closer to Willa, inclined his head. His lips hovered above her ear, his hands above her waist, his thumbs above her ribcage.

"I'm not sure, but from where I stand you seem to be receiving loud and clear."

She looked up into his eyes, then, his face but inches away. His lashes were too long and too lazy, his expression rife with flirtation and fun, his smile filled with endless and exciting possibilities. A low moan escaped Willa's throat and Joel's hands made contact.

Softly, she laughed, amazed how this attraction between them had so quickly blossomed. But this was neither the time nor the place and they'd do best to keep the moment light and playful before the tension escalated and Joel's hands moved higher.

Willa took a deep breath, inhaling the warmth and aroused scent of Joel. It was hard to think straight after that. But the sudden muffled snore of the sleeping baby caught her attention and turned their two's company into three's a crowd.

She blinked slowly, met Joel's smoky gaze. "It seems your munchkin is down for the count."

Joel frowned, focused, looked toward the place where Leigh had settled to play. He shook his head and smiled. "Like I said, anytime—"

"Anywhere." Moving away from his tempting mouth, Willa finished his thought on her way to the closet where she found another tote bag and the safety of distance. "I'm going to pack up her clothes while she's out."

"Right. Yeah. We need to get moving." Joel backed toward the door. He jerked a thumb over his shoulder. "I'll just go check on Shadow."

Nodding, she pulled open a drawer and found one-piece rompers. "Good idea. This shouldn't take me long."

"You need help?"

She shook her head, smiled, kept her eyes on her task. "I'm fine."

"All right then. I'll be out back if you need me." And then he was gone.

Willa slumped against the closet door, glad the room contained a crib and not anything larger of the bed variety. Because what she hadn't been ready for last night, she was definitely ready for now.

# Get
# FREE BOOKS
## and a wonderful
# FREE GIFT!

**Try Your Luck At Our Casino, Where All The Games Are On The House!**

## PLAY ROULETTE!

## PLAY TWENTY-ONE

*Turn the page and deal yourself in!*

# WELCOME TO THE
# CASINO!

## Try your luck at the Roulette Wheel ...
## Play a hand of Twenty-One!

### How to play:

1. Play the Roulette and Twenty-One scratch-off games, as instructed on the opposite page, to see that you are eligible for FREE BOOKS and a FREE GIFT!

2. Send back the card and you'll receive TWO brand-new Harlequin Temptation® novels. These books have a cover price of $3.75 each in the U.S. and $4.25 each in Canada, but they are yours to keep absolutely free.

3. There's no catch. You're under no obligation to buy anything. We charge nothing — ZERO — for your first shipment. And you don't have to make any minimum number of purchases — not even one!

4. The fact is, thousands of readers enjoy receiving books by mail from the Harlequin Reader Service® before they're available in stores. They like the convenience of home delivery, and they love our discount prices!

5. We hope that after receiving your free books you'll want to remain a subscriber. But the choice is yours — to continue or cancel, any time at all!

So why not take us up on our invitation, with no risk of any kind. You'll be glad you did!

## Play Twenty-One For This Exquisite Free Gift!

### THIS SURPRISE
### MYSTERY GIFT
### WILL BE YOURS
### FREE WHEN YOU PLAY
### TWENTY-ONE

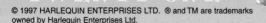

# It's fun, and we're giving away *FREE GIFTS* to all players!

## PLAY ROULETTE!

Scratch the silver to see that the ball has landed on 7 RED, making you eligible for TWO FREE romance novels!

## PLAY TWENTY-ONE!

Scratch the silver to reveal a winning hand! Congratulations, you have Twenty-One. Return this card promptly and you'll receive a fabulous free mystery gift, along with your free books!

## YES!

Please send me all the free Harlequin Temptation® books and the gift for which I qualify! I understand that I am under no obligation to purchase any books, as explained on the back of this card.

Name: _____

(PLEASE PRINT)

Address: _____ Apt.#: _____

City: _____ State: _____ Zip: _____

# The Harlequin Reader Service® — Here's how it works:

Accepting your 2 free books and mystery gift places you under no obligation to buy anything. You may keep the books and gift and return the shipping statement marked "cancel." If you do not cancel, about a month later we'll send you 4 additional novels and bill you just $3.12 each in the U.S., or $3.57 each in Canada, plus 25¢ delivery per book and applicable taxes if any.* That's the complete price and — compared to the cover price of $3.75 in the U.S. and $4.25 in Canada — it's quite a bargain! You may cancel at any time, but if you choose to continue, every month we'll send you 4 more books, which you may either purchase at the discount price or return to us and cancel your subscription.

*Terms and prices subject to change without notice. Sales tax applicable in N.Y. Canadian residents will be charged applicable provincial taxes and GST.

HOW A TEN-MONTH-OLD managed to get dirt in every crease of skin from head to toe, Joel would never understand. But somehow Scout had succeeded.

Standing in front of his linen closet, he bounced her on one hip in an attempt to keep her awake long enough for a bath and a bottle.

It had been a long day for all of them.

He'd walked into Jen's backyard and found Shadow with no food and no water. The dog had been lying in a hole freshly dug beneath the cedar privacy fence in an apparent attempt to escape starvation and solitary confinement.

With a vow to return for a piece of Howie Jr.'s irresponsible teenage hide, Joel had loaded the muddy retriever into the bed of the pickup. Willa walked out of Jen's house minutes later and, after fastening the baby securely in her car seat, had calmed the excited dog and suggested they skip their planned lunch stop and make a beeline for home.

Leigh had been vocally adamant about getting her hands on her pet, straining around in her seat to see out the cab's rear window and making the drive an experience Joel would just as soon not repeat. Once they arrived at Willa's place, he'd finally given in, figuring at the worst he'd have to reimburse Jen for a ruined pair of red Winnie-The-Pooh pajamas.

After a quick lunch, he and Scout had spent the rest of the afternoon at the kennels with Willa where all five dogs received her attention. Joel had pitched in, cleaning the pens while Willa made quick work of baths and grooming. The hours gave him a firsthand taste of the exhausting pace her profession required as well as the exacting performance she required of herself.

Leigh had watched from the sidelines, in her Exersaucer, clapping her hands and calling out to the dogs as each was put through its routine. But afternoon had become evening and, though Joel had fed lunch to the munchkin, she became cranky with hunger and the need to sleep.

He hadn't wanted to come home. Not because his seduction was progressing and he hated to leave, but because he enjoyed Willa's company.

He had a responsibility to his niece and his sister, however. So, he'd have to be satisfied knowing he'd see Willa tomorrow. And he'd make it a point to do so.

Scout snuggled her sleepy head into his neck. Smiling, he dropped a kiss on her cheek. He loved this baby. He couldn't imagine loving one of his own more than he did this child of his sister's.

His family was a bachelor's dream. They offered loving support—even in his decision to live his life alone. Because of that, in fact, they were there for him probably more than they would've been if he had a wife to come home to each night.

He spent a lot of his days off with his dad. They fished. They golfed. Recently, they'd even begun rebuilding a short-block Chevy engine. Joel enjoyed those times. It gave him a chance to talk, really talk, with his father.

But it was Jen with whom he talked about relationships. Not that he sought her out for that purpose. His sister happened to be all woman, able to pry out thoughts and dreams and feelings he never even admitted to himself.

She was the one who understood best why he didn't want children. She respected his decision, admired his conviction. Or so she said. It was what she didn't say, the words she left unspoken that were the hardest to hear.

Jen had found such happiness with Rob, she wanted the same for her brother. And she had trouble accepting that Joel could be happy with the status quo when he hadn't experienced such a partnership as the one she shared with her husband—one that had produced the precious child curled up against Joel's chest.

God, what would he have done if something had happened yesterday to Leigh? How would he have explained his actions to Jen? Jen being Jen, she'd never have blamed him. She would've grieved and blamed the teen duo, the store clerk, the time of day and the weather.

But then she wouldn't have had to place blame where blame belonged. Joel would've done that, blamed himself enough for both of them, blamed himself for thinking like a cop instead of like Leigh's uncle.

He blew out a snort. Thinking like a cop. As if he knew how to think any other way. He obviously didn't. He would've thought of the danger to both Leigh and Willa if he knew how to think like a friend or an uncle.

Damn.

As much as he'd enjoyed Willa's company today and was looking forward to tomorrow, he still hadn't gotten over yesterday, the day they'd spent together, the way they'd appeared—to more than one person—to be a couple.

That would mean he and Willa had shared the type of looks that passed between Jen and Rob. That he and Willa had given off vibes that strangers had picked up on.

He wasn't exactly at ease with the fact that they'd achieved a comfort level that a lot of committed couples took serious time reaching. It implied an intimacy they shouldn't have shared without being, well, intimate.

Not that intimacy was long in coming. Her body had been ready last night, but her mind had still needed time. Judging by her response—and her comments—in the nursery earlier today, Willa had spent the past twenty-four hours deep in thought. Joel liked that. He liked that a lot.

He wasn't sure what to make of Willa's confession, or if he understood why she'd told him of her accident. Was it to reassure him that pregnancy wouldn't be a problem? And that she hadn't had a lover in a very long time?

That seemed to be the most logical reason, the only one with any bearing on whatever relationship they might have. Hmm. Joel shifted Leigh to his opposite shoulder. "Might have" was a poor choice of words, he mused, as confidence brought a smile to his mouth.

"Might" left open a door of doubt about what would happen between him and Willa. And there wasn't a doubt in his mind about what would happen, what was going to happen, what he couldn't wait to happen.

And even as prurient thoughts crossed his mind, a shadow crossed the hallway.

"DO YOU NEED some help?"

Willa walked down the hall to where Joel stood with his niece against his shoulder, the baby dozing, then startling herself awake each time he moved. She'd showered and changed and hurried over, knowing Joel had a very sleepy—not to mention dirty—baby on his hands.

He offered Willa the strangest grin, almost as if he'd been thinking about her before she'd appeared. "You can help me get Scout here into the tub before she passes out on me."

"I have a better idea." She reached past him, snatched up a towel, a bottle of liquid baby bath and headed for the kitchen. Joel followed, stepping into the room as she squared the terry cloth on the counter next to the sink. "Make it an adventure and she'll stay awake and curious long enough to get clean."

"You're going to bathe her in the sink?"

*Men.* "Think of it as a munchkin-sized bathtub. Same composition as the one you bathe in, just smaller. And waist level. Easier on your leg and all."

"Practical. I like that in a woman."

She set the baby on the towel, adjusted the water temperature and stripped Joel's niece down to her diaper while the sink filled. Leigh's giggles began the minute the first soap bubbles popped inches from her nose. She poked chubby fingers into the suds and squealed her delight with the froth.

Willa made quick work of bathing the baby. At

least, as quick as she could considering Leigh seemed to have decided this was the most fun she'd had all day, and Joel seemed determined to egg her on.

Willa finally shrugged out of her flannel. She tossed the shirt to the kitchen floor before more than the cuffs ended up as wet as the baby in the sink.

Joel leaned into the elbow he'd propped on the countertop and splashed water over Leigh's back. The baby responded with a hard slap of both hands onto the water's surface.

Water splattered the front of Willa's tank and Joel's black T-shirt. She yelped and sputtered and glared in his direction, droplets dangling from her lashes. He, of course, was the poster child for boyish innocence.

"The Wolfsleys are suckers for water sports," he said, a fat droplet plopping from the end of his nose to his upper lip.

"So I see." She swiped the back of her hand across her cheek, tempted within an inch of her life to return the wet favor his way. The way Joel's gaze swept over her, lingering on her damp tank before seeking out her eyes tempted her further.

But then he looked back at Leigh and snorted, bursting the bubble of the moment. "I'll be so glad to get out of this." He knocked on the cast. "It took me forever to figure the easiest way to shower without soaking the damn thing. By the time I'm mobile again, I'll have the technique down pat."

Willa thought about Joel's technique. She thought about his shower. She thought about the day behind them leading up to the night ahead.

She finished rinsing the baby, lifted her onto the towel and wrapped her to dry.

Then she looked at Joel and said, "That's what I'm here for. To help."

He stopped breathing, then pulled in a ragged breath and slowly shoved it out between clenched teeth. His control wavered and seemed to mirror the anxious feelings that closed her throat and made breathing near impossible. She'd been waiting for this night forever.

"For now, though," she added when a vein at his temple throbbed. "Why don't you take this one, get her dried and dressed while I fix her a bottle."

Taking the baby from Willa's arms, Joel nodded, grimly silent as he left the room. It wasn't the grim of dark thoughts, or worry or studied concentration. No, it was the grim of frustration that responsibility came before fun.

Willa knew all this because the same set of jaw and tightly drawn mouth was making her face hurt. She shook it off and turned back to the bath leftovers, wiping down the sink and countertop then fixing a bottle.

And Willa's timing was perfect. Joel limped back into the kitchen just then with his niece clad in pink cotton, her cheeks rosy, her hair brushed back in damp ringlets. His expression had calmed, but remained intent as he took the bottle Willa offered.

He'd stripped off his shirt, which had suffered a fair drenching, and he leaned back against the refrigerator, holding the baby to his chest. Leigh snuggled close, her sleepy eyes held wide open by sheer will. She studied Joel's face, her bottle in one hand, the tiny fingers of the other weaving through the dusting of chest hair tickling her cheek.

Willa couldn't help but appreciate Joel's physical beauty. His shoulders were body-builder wide without the excessive bulk that often came with that obsession. His chest was broad, muscled, covered with fine hair that tapered below his sternum into a darker line that disappeared behind Leigh's lower half. Willa caught a brief glimpse of the stripe at Joel's low-riding waistband before she realized where had gaze had wandered.

She let it wander still, wondering about his leg and the suffering from his injury. If it pained him still. How long it would be before he regained the strength so apparent in his good leg. The one muscled and firm, filling out the denim of his jeans as it bore the brunt of his weight.

The picture he made was one Willa knew would stay with her long after tonight. It was a color snapshot, a greeting card, the Big Bad Wolf and the baby captured forever in her mind.

And it came to Willa then that one day there would be another woman savoring moments such as this one. That she wouldn't be the one sharing them with Joel. He wouldn't be her husband and she wouldn't have a child sending this warmth through her body, a warmth that blossomed into a sense that this world, this man, offered the safest of harbors.

A deep breath steadied her fanciful mood. She was here for the moment, not the future. She needed desperately to keep that in mind or else the road leading into the night would be paved with so

much disaster and none of the uncomplicated pleasure that seemed forever in coming.

"Criminy, Willa. Keep looking at me that way
and I'm liable to drop Scout here."

Willa let her gaze crawl back up Joel's body to
his face. His arousal in no way escaped her notice.
In fact, her notice lingered longer than decorum or
Miss Manners would deem proper. But neither
was it proper for her to want to touch him the way
she did. The way she was going to. Right now.

She stepped closer, feeling the heat of his body
as she moved into his space. "You're not going to
drop your niece, Joel."

"Then how 'bout I drop my pants?"

Willa tossed back her head and laughed. She felt
so good, so full of all things female. "I don't think
that's a good idea."

"Why not? I think it's a damn good idea."

"Because in about three minutes Leigh is going
to be out." The baby's lashes barely fluttered at the
mention of her name. "And then you'd be stuck in
a bind worse than the one you seem to be in now."

"Bind isn't even the half of it." He handed Willa
the bottle, which had fallen from Leigh's hand and
now lay on her chest. Then he shifted the sleeping
baby to his shoulder.

Joel's broad hand spanned the width of Leigh's
back, his other arm supported her rump. Her lips
had parted against his shoulder as she settled into
the untroubled sleep of innocence.

Willa crossed her arms over her chest and smiled
up at Joel. "You're a natural, you know."

"Yeah. The perfect nanny. Mary Poppins and
Fran Drescher rolled up into one."

"I was thinking more along the lines of daddy."

"Come closer, little girl." He crooked one finger. "I'll be your daddy."

She did come closer. And closer still. A step at a time until they were separated by the baby he held. Willa crooked her own finger. And then she ran the back of her knuckle down the front of his stomach, beneath his navel, where the waist of his jeans rode low. "You're a sexy man, Joel Wolfsley."

He sucked in air through his teeth. "You just like the way my pants fit."

"I like that you have a sense of humor."

"Ranks right up there with my great personality."

He hissed as her hand began to move, glanced up at the ceiling, squeezed his eyes tight as her finger slipped beneath his waistband, looked back once his control was marginally regained. "Forget the personals ad and stick with the getting personal, will ya?"

"Personals ad, huh? Hmm." She continued the slow rub of her knuckle over his skin. "I'm not sure I'd answer that one. Cute, but not a lot of substance. What about long walks on the beach? Candlelit dinners? Ballroom dancing?"

"Ballroom dancing?" One brow arched. The same side of his mouth crooked up wryly. "Sorry. I'm all outta legs. These days I dance best flat on my back."

Willa rolled her eyes. "That was terrible."

"It was bad, wasn't it?" His expression grew serious then. His eyes darkened, summer green turning to a winter forest pine. "But not as bad as the way I want to make love to you."

# 8

JOEL WASN'T SURE how they'd made it to his bedroom, only that they had. He wasn't going to complain about the trip, not now when they were finally here. Sure, he'd've loved to have wrapped Willa's naked legs around his waist and kissed her senseless the length of the hallway.

But he wasn't a miracle worker. What he was was in a cast. Keeping himself upright when his motor control had been cut off by his libido's jet engine, well…he wouldn't have passed a sobriety test if he'd been asked to walk a straight line.

And even if he had been stone-cold sober and able to stand arrow straight, Willa was wearing work boots and jeans, and he couldn't handle either of those with any measure of finesse.

Not that the sweet talking of a first time necessarily guaranteed smooth moves. The opposite was usually the case. The guy came fast because, well, hell, he couldn't take the wait any longer. And the lady—because he didn't have experience with any females who weren't true ladies—was more often than not a bunch of nerves about doing the *right thing* and didn't come at all.

Joel might not be able to sweep Willa off her feet or strip her naked without her noticing his sleight of hand, but he would damn sure make her come.

"You weren't lying, were you?" she asked.

She stood in front of him, facing the bed, holding her flannel shirt to her chest. Nuzzling the shell of her ear from behind, he reached over her shoulder and tossed the shirt to the floor. Then he reached for the hem of her tank. He took the shirt off over her head then pulled her back into his body and, biting down hard on a shiver, savored her warm and soft and supplely female skin.

Still savoring, he followed the direction of her gaze—toward his headboard from which a dozen pair of handcuffs dangled. Complete with keys, each was shackled to the narrow railing by one bracelet. No, he hadn't lied. But right now he didn't want to explain the history of the collection.

He growled low in her ear and said, "The better to have my way with you."

"Is that so?" She dropped a light kiss on the forearm hugging her collarbone inches above her breasts.

"Or," he added with a bit of a chuckle. "The better for you to have your way with me."

Leaning her head back against his shoulder, she brushed fingertips over the tiny mark she'd left on his skin. "I think I'd like to have my way with you. But first…"

No. No firsts. "First?"

"Will you tell me what you want me to do?"

The invitation was every man's dream and left Joel speechless. At that moment, he couldn't remember having ever wanted a woman with this degree of possessive fierceness. It bothered him. A lot.

But it didn't keep him from saying, "What I

want you to do is simple. Let me make love to you."

Willa stared back at him over her shoulder, her gaze confused yet satisfied, her mouth a spoiled pout. "That defeats the purpose of the question, doesn't it?"

"Baby, right now I don't give a damn about the question. Only about the answer." Her head was still tilted back. Her bound ponytail brushed his skin.

Feeling her hair against his bare chest was torture. He hissed out a low breath. "If I don't get inside you and quick, I'm afraid I'm gonna go off."

She kept the line of her mouth straight, but he knew it wasn't easy. He knew that because when she turned in his arms to face him, he saw that she'd caught her lower lip between her teeth to hold back her grin.

Of course, she couldn't hold it long. "Are you saying we may be dealing with an accidental shooting?"

He grinned, drew fingers down her spine, stopped when he reached her jeans-covered bottom and squeezed. "Does the term *weapon misfire* mean anything to you?"

Her blue eyes flashed with humor and the recognition that she was about to take a cop to bed. "I suppose you're looking to holster that weapon?"

"Well now, Darlin'. I'd better do just that." He squeezed again. Both hands. Both buttocks. "Or else we'll be dealing with the consequences of a little friendly fire."

Willa threw back her head and laughed. "You need help."

If anything, he was about to need a mop and a bucket because her breasts were rubbing against his chest and now her fingers were moving.

And they were moving over his skin. And they were unbuttoning the copper buttons that barely held his fly together. And when she'd finished with the buttons and stopped moving, he had a hard time not jerking his pants to the ground.

"Joel?"

"Willa?"

She looked up. "I have a problem."

*She* had a problem? "Anything I can do to help?"

"I'm having trouble with your pants."

The trouble was that she didn't have them off yet. "What kind of trouble?"

"I'm afraid I'm not going to be able to get them down. I've run into an—" she tilted her head to one side and frowned "—an obstacle."

What she'd run into was his hard-on. "Trust me. It's...surmountable."

She rolled her eyes at that. "I'm sure it is. You got your pants on, after all."

Joel frowned. They were either suffering a serious miscommunication here or he was more impressive than he'd thought.

"I mean, I can get them down to your knees without a hitch," Willa continued. "But I'm not quite sure what to do after that."

His cast. She was talking about his cast while he was talking about parts of his body that were as hard as the navy fiberglass. "Ah, that's easy. An old stripper's trick."

And then he ripped open the pants leg from the point above his knee to his crotch.

Willa smiled. "Velcro?"

"Pretty cool, huh? The wife of a buddy at work fixed me up."

"This is great," Willa said, fingering the hidden closure.

"Yep. Four pairs of my jeans are now ready for show time on the Richmond Strip." He did a little bump and grind.

"I like it. I like it a lot," she said and ran her fingertips up his bare inner thigh to the leg of his briefs. "But I do have one more question."

And one more answer was probably all he had left before his knees buckled. "One. That's it."

"It's okay, isn't it? If I make love to you, too?" Her eyes were wide and blue and honest and more giving than he'd ever expected.

He hissed out a long, low, frustrated impatient breath. He knew what they were making here wasn't about love, but it sure as hell didn't feel like just sex. "As long as you know that what happens here this first time isn't…well…"

And after all the promises he'd made to himself, he was going to blow it. He'd be doing good to last about as long as a randy virgin schoolboy.

"Isn't, well, what?" She'd slipped her fingers into his shorts now and was feeling up his backside.

He was going to have to stop her before she made it around to his front. "I need to be inside you, Willa. Now. It won't be slow and romantic. Not this time."

"You don't have to woo me, Joel. I'm here. And I want to feel you inside me probably as much as you want to be there."

He wasn't sure how to respond to that, but if she felt even half the need ripping open his gut, this was gonna be a hell of a coming together. "So, you think we can get busy here? Or do you need directions?"

"Directions?" She gave him a know-it-all lift of her brows. "Like how to slide tab A into slot B?"

"Mmm. Something like that."

"You want directions? I'll give you directions." She spun him around and pushed him back down onto the mattress. "Down is a direction, right?"

"So's up," he said and thrust his hips that way.

"Up? Like this?" Leaning forward she ran her palms over his fly and up his belly. He squirmed in the bed, pushing back farther on the mattress so that if she decided to straddle him she'd have a place to put her knees. He just hoped she took both their pants off first.

Her hands continued up his sides, over his armpits, his triceps, to his elbows, forearms, wrists, palms, lacing her fingers through his when she reached his hands which were now high over his head. She shifted on the bed until she was doing that straddle thing he'd been waiting for.

Even with her pants on it wasn't far from heaven, feeling her over him, her breasts suspended just out of reach of his mouth. His tongue wasn't quite long enough to do more than flick lightly across her bare nipples when he wanted to draw her deep into his mouth.

She drew deep on him instead, teasing his mouth with light nips and love bites before kissing him full and hard like he wanted to be kissed, with her tongue and her body, both of which he was getting impatient to feel elsewhere.

And then, while he was doing his best to kiss her senseless in return, while he was working to coax her into getting naked so they could get this show on the road, she snapped handcuffs around both his wrists.

With a kiss dropped first on his forehead, then his nose, his chin, center chest and low on his stomach, she hopped up off the bed and left him there.

"Willa?" He called after her when she left the room.

"Don't go anywhere, Joel. I'll be right back."

Oh, she was a funny girl, this one. But she hadn't gone far. He heard her banging cabinet doors, slamming drawers in the kitchen. Then all was quiet and Joel realized he was half-naked with a hard-on and handcuffed to his own bed.

*Paradise.*

Of course, he probably wouldn't have been so cocky if he'd truly been trapped. But since each pair of handcuffs hung from the headboard by one bracelet and he was caught in the dangling cuffs of two separate pairs, well, it would be easy to slide his hands together and open either set.

He only considered it for half a second, then decided to hang around instead and see what Willa had in mind.

A minute or two more and she returned wearing nothing but her white cotton bikinis and tank top. Joel's heart slammed to the back of his chest.

Her legs were long anyway, but those high cut panties seemed to add another six inches. The curve of her hip was sweet. He'd thought she might be more lean, more…solid and straight, but her muscles were all female. Nothing boyish here about her figure.

But what struck him most about her—even more than her legs, her strong arms and great shoulders, or even the way her breasts were as arousing now as they had been inches from his mouth—was her hair. This was the first time he'd ever seen it down.

She'd brought two pie tins back to the bedroom with her, along with his box of squat emergency candles. As she went about setting the tins on his dresser on either side of the mirror, her hair swung about her shoulders. Once she had a half dozen of the plain white votives burning in their shiny metal bases, she flipped off the bright light overhead.

Shadows flickered as the flames ate up the wicks. The mirror reflected the tongues of light back into the room, and over Willa's hair. She turned to face him, leaned back against his dresser, framed on both her right and her left by the flames.

Her hair was fair and colorless in the subdued glow, yet the light played the part of an artist's brush and turned the strands to gold. He needed to remember to tell her how much he liked it down, how good she looked wearing candlelight and white.

But he wasn't sure he'd be able to coherently remember much of anything at all because right then she smiled.

And while she was smiling she worked off his single athletic shoe and one sock. His jeans, already opened, slid down his legs freely.

He'd only thought he'd found paradise half-naked with a hard-on and handcuffed to his own bed.

Paradise wasn't even the half of it.

This was like a fantasy he'd forgotten to create back when he was still conjuring fantasies that involved being at a woman's tender mercy. And this fantasy was getting better because Willa had a bottle in her hand.

Joel squirmed as she shot a stream of Leigh's creamy baby oil onto one palm and then climbed onto the bed and knelt between his legs. "Uh, Willa?"

"Yes, Joel?

"What're you up to down there, Baby?"

She answered with her hands and Joel sucked in a sharp breath as the warmth hit his skin. The lotion was heated; Willa's hands were cool. Both sensations were a shock to his system.

The experience would have been enough to kill a weaker man. But Joel wasn't weak.

Or so he reminded himself as Willa's palms stroked upward on his thighs, down to his knees, up again and down. She squeezed out more lotion and started in again by rubbing her thumbs hard over his abs, moving to his ribcage, working her hands up his sides and back to his belly, never quite taking her massage to the part of his body most needing to be stroked.

Eyes closed, he gave up fighting for control of his mind or his body. And why shouldn't he? Willa was obviously determined to do everything he'd've asked her to do if he'd had the patience to make a list.

By the time she finished with his arms, his body

was one big nerve ending reaching for the sky. He couldn't concentrate. He couldn't think beyond the moment. He wasn't even sure he could move.

And then she kissed him. Right through the cotton of the one and only clothing item she'd left him wearing. Without any sort of hesitation, she opened her mouth and breathed a trail of hot kisses along the throbbing bulge in his shorts.

Joel jerked against the handcuffs, forgetting that she had him where she wanted him. Forgetting, also, that seconds ago he'd given up fighting himself. Forgetting everything he'd ever known when she lowered the elastic band of his shorts, pulled them off and to the floor and tasted his bare skin.

The kiss deepened, grew intimately erotic until her lips enclosed him completely. And then her hand was moving over him, spreading the wetness left by her mouth to places high and low, spreading, too, his need for release. He had to stop her now. Before this was over too soon.

As if she'd read his mind, she stopped herself. He was breathing hard and throbbing hard and the cool air after her warm mouth made him shake. Either that or he'd become a mindless mass of raw nerve endings. Whatever, he couldn't do much beyond watch and drool when she moved up his body.

With her knees on either side of his waist, she raised up and shucked off her tank. Her panties were the next to go. He wasn't sure how she managed without ever fully leaving the bed or his lap, but she did, in a shimmy sort of move, down the hips, over the knee and calf, off the foot, then the same routine repeated.

She was so beautiful, there above him, naked and gorgeously full and female. He wanted to touch her, to feel the soft skin and hair between her legs. He wanted to look at her, to taste her, to enjoy her with all of his senses.

Suddenly, he didn't want to rush this at all because he knew no matter how long they loved it wouldn't be long enough. Even knowing there'd be hours to spend with Willa later didn't lessen his desire to get this time right.

And as that thought pleased him, Willa pleased him, sliding slowly onto his erection, bracing her hands on the mattress beneath his shoulders. Once he was fully sheathed, she came to a stop atop him. Dipping down, she ran her tongue flat over one nipple, moved to the other.

Joel came up off the bed. He wasn't going to be able to get close enough, get deep enough, not without his hands free to hold her, to guide her as she rode.

She rode him well, moving up and moving down and moving hard against him. She fit him well, tightening her muscles as she stroked his body with hers. She loved him well, drawing out his pleasure, following the instructions he gave physically, silently with commands of hips and thighs.

He waited for her to come. He felt her grow ready, felt her body's building reaction to the pleasure she found in his, felt that flow of female electricity as she relinquished control.

And then he couldn't feel anything beyond the release she drew from his body. He poured into her, filled her, shuddered as his will lost out to the male animal that was his body. Sexuality took over in a burst of raw energy and he pushed up against her, giving her all he had to give.

It was long minutes before either of them moved, Willa resting on his chest, Joel lifting his knees behind her to hold her there. He was still full and she remained tight around him and when he playfully thrust upward, she grinned into the base of his neck.

"Again?" she mumbled.

He thrust twice. "Just say when."

She used her palms to push herself upward and sat, her body still a part of his. "I was thinking about taking a shower first."

"No you weren't. You were thinking about taking a shower at the same time."

"Wicked man."

He shook his head in disagreement. "Wicked woman."

"Trust me. My seeming wickedness is all your fault."

"My fault?" He exaggerated his frown, lifted arms that were growing cramped. "And next you'll be claiming I did this to myself?"

"That—" she nodded toward the handcuffs "—was self-preservation."

"Do unto others before they do unto you?"

"I didn't hear you complain." She crossed her arms beneath her breasts and double dared him to make the next move.

"I'm not the complaining type." He slid his wrists together and opened the handcuffs in turn. "And I never surrender the upper hand."

Willa's jaw dropped. Then she narrowed both

eyes and gave a playful smack to his chest. "You'll pay for that one, Wolfsley."

He wasn't fast enough to catch her. She came up off his lap and scampered to the bathroom, leaving her hand print above his heart, which was strangely aching already.

"YOU WERE GREAT." Willa had just come back from checking on Leigh and had curled up against Joel's side, pulling the sheet and quilt up under her chin.

After they'd shared what had to rank right up there at the top of his list of life's memorable moments, Willa had carried through on her promise to help him bathe.

Not that there had been much bathing done. They'd cleaned up the mess they'd made before showering as well as the one they'd made while he'd stood half in, half out of the spray. But bathing? Nope. Not a lot of that had been done.

Man, what a couple of days he'd had. First had been the sprint and endurance events chasing after Leigh. Then had come the marathon with Willa. She was right. He had been great.

He was also exhausted.

"I *was* good, wasn't I?" Might as well bask in her glory. "For a few minutes there I wasn't sure which one of us was howling at the moon."

"That would be the one of us with 'wolf' in his name." She nuzzled up to his chin which he'd meant to scrape clean in the shower. "The same one with maybe a bit of 'wolf' in his blood, as well."

"Only when it's a full moon. Or when a she-wolf claims him as her mate."

"I did no such thing."

Her indignation tickled him and Joel lifted the edge of the sheet. The full moon threw stripes of light through the open mini-blinds across his chest. He pointed out the teeth marks.

Willa squirreled down beneath the covers.

"Uh-huh. Don't pull that shy routine on me. I know you, remember?"

He knew he'd said the wrong thing the minute the words left his mouth. Willa stilled and grew pensive, her eyes searched his and her heart beat hard against his side.

Joel refused to panic, but neither was he going to spend the night sleeping with Willa *and* her doubts. "Spit it out, Willa. What's on your mind?"

She lifted away the foot she'd been rubbing across his calf. "I was just thinking that we know each other as neighbors, yes. But we've never been close friends."

He'd been expecting this. But later. After a bit of distance. After she'd had time to think. "We shouldn't be here, you mean."

"It's not so much that..." She turned onto her stomach, raised up on both elbows, looked down at the pillow instead of his way. "When I said you were great, I wasn't talking about this, with us. I was talking about the other day. At the store."

*Oh. That.* "Which store? We stopped at several."

"You know what I'm talking about." She plucked at a hair on his chest.

He rubbed at the sting. "Yeah, I do. I figured you'd get around to that soon enough."

"You don't want to talk about it?" she asked, and this time she looked at him. Intently. Intensely.

Intelligently searching beyond his eyes for all the reasons why.

How could she know so much about him in such a short short time? Joel was the first to glance away. He stared at the mirror, the reflected candle-light. "What's to talk about? It happened. It's over."

She blew out a disgusted, disbelieving huff of breath. "Joel, you can't seriously be that blasé."

"I'm not being blasé." He rolled to his side and propped up on one elbow. The move raised him above Willa's upturned face. Gazing down at her he felt the return of his sense of control. He went on. "That's what I do for a living. That's who I am. A cop. I rough up the bad guys and get paid for it."

Her smile started slowly, working it's way from her all-seeing eyes to the corners of the mouth that challenged him with a return volley of his own words, until Joel found himself facing that thing all men fear: a woman too wise.

"You were great, Joel."

He'd maneuvered his way into the upper hand, or at least the upper position. And with four words spoken, four simple words delivered to the heart of their target, she was right back on top.

He dropped a kiss to the tip of her nose. "That's Detective Wolfsley to you."

"Detective Wolfsley." She nodded in a mocking sort of bow. "You were so in control. So calm. It looked almost...what's the word? Routine. But I know it can't be. You wouldn't be in a cast if your job was routine."

"Not true," he said, shaking his head. "A lot of days what I do is about as routine as tossing burgers on a grill. But sure, it's a routine with more than a few drawbacks. There's not a job that doesn't have at least one or two."

Her brow came up. "Flipping burgers?"

"Sure. Undercooking. Overcooking. All that grease."

"Those are hardly drawbacks."

"Depends on whose burger it is you screw up." She rolled her eyes and Joel laughed. "You gotta weigh the disadvantages against the good stuff, Willa. You're a hell of a dog lady, but you still run the risk of meeting up with some bad canine teeth. I'm a hell of a cop. But that doesn't mean I'm never going to run across a junkie desperate enough to use a car as a weapon."

"Is that what happened?" Her voice was thready and high. And it fairly squeaked when she added, "A hit and run?"

He'd boxed himself into this one all right. And he didn't see but one honest way out. "A little more involved than a hit and run. Attempted murder of a police officer."

If there'd been a better source of light in the room, Joel knew he would have seen Willa pale. He didn't need light to feel her limbs grow cold. Or to feel the knife of regret cutting a deep valley in his gut.

It hadn't been his intention to frighten her, but her fear made a good argument for the distance he kept, for the reason he remained single. He couldn't, wouldn't subject a woman he loved to the sort of pain that came with caring in the face of constant danger.

She was calm but still cold when she asked,

"He's in jail now, right? This guy who tried to ki...this guy who hit you?"

The Dark Knight of the Dark City, as the drug lord had christened himself, was known to law officers across southeast Texas as The Knight. And, no, he wasn't in jail, which had been partly responsible for his reluctance to keep Leigh. He never underestimated a dealer out for revenge. One who valued product over property and valued life not at all.

"Not yet. But cop killers tend to get—" how best to put this to a woman who didn't live the ins and outs of the force "—special treatment. He won't be free for long."

"Will he come after you?"

"I don't know, Willa. I pretty much kicked The Knight's network out from under him. He lost the product he had to sell and lost his buyers for anything else he's able to put his hands on. It takes time to build the system he had. It's a sick sort of trust, but then it's a sick existence."

"Doesn't that frighten you?"

"What frightens me is knowing that if he's not caught soon, he'll be back in business and people will die. That's what frightens me most of all."

She was silent and Joel felt the clawing discomfort of the long moment. Then she whispered, "More than the idea of your own death? At his hand?"

"Like I said, I'm a hell of a good cop." Time to change the direction of this conversation. He didn't like the sound of Willa's voice. Or the faraway look on her face. He wanted her here. He wanted her now.

"I'm trained to handle the unexpected. Just like you know what to do when an owner drops off an uncontrollable shoe-chewing dog." He skated his fingers down her bare back.

"That's different."

"Why? I know how to deal with dangerous people. Your experience is with dangerous animals."

"I'm not buying it, Joel. You can hardly compare the two."

"I'm not comparing the two."

"Yes—"

"No." He cut her off. "I'm comparing competency. Yours and mine. I wouldn't know the first thing about dealing with a wild dog. And if I'd sent you in to pay for today's gas, you'd have walked right past the kid outside and into a lot of trouble."

"You're right. I would have. But I watched you. And I knew something wasn't right. And even after I put the clues together and figured it out, I wasn't scared."

She turned to her side and faced him belly to breast. "That's what I meant about you doing good, Joel. And about making it look routine. I felt safe with you. I wasn't scared at all."

"You were scared, Willa. I saw your hands shaking when you reached for my gun."

"What I was frightened of was the unknown. But I never feared for my safety. Or for Leigh's. In fact, the only time I felt uneasy was in the timing of my 911 call."

"You did fine."

"But I hesitated. I didn't want to raise the hood of the truck. I didn't want to block my line of sight.

Because that would've kept me from being able to see you.''

She lowered her lashes, lifted them slowly and Joel swore he saw a glimmer of tears in her eyes.

Damn.

This wasn't how their relationship was supposed to work. Hadn't that been in their contract? Wasn't this about sex and nothing more? She hadn't cried before, during or after the holdup. So, why was she about to cry now? And why was she about to cry over him?

Damn.

He didn't want a permanent relationship. She hoped one day her prince would come. They'd talked about physical needs and the complications and consequences of taking a lover.

He and Willa should've been perfect for one another.

The problem was…they were.

## 9

"YOU TWO ARE lifesavers. I owe both of you, big time." Jennifer took her daughter from her brother's arms and hugged the baby close, rubbing her nose against the soft skin of Leigh's neck and inhaling the sweetness. "I can't believe Mom and Dad still haven't come home."

"Well, now, you know Mom and Dad—" Joel started to say, only to be cut off by Jennifer's playful smack on the arm. He rubbed at the spot with a petulant, "Hey."

"Yes. I do know Mom and Dad," she said to her brother then turned to Willa. "Long-running sibling joke. Our parents are so predictably unpredictable. I was just so anxious to get to Rob that I didn't stop to think how often they change their plans."

"That'll teach you to think with your brain instead of your—" Jennifer raised a sisterly brow and Joel let the thought trail, picking it up again with, "So, how *is* Rob?"

"Very happy to see his wife. And very grateful that we have a sitter we can implicitly trust." She raised up on tiptoes to brush a kiss across Joel's cheek. "Thank you Wolf Man. Seriously. And you, too, Willa," she added, shifting Leigh to her opposite hip. "I certainly didn't mean to be such a bother. I'd like to make it up to you somehow."

Standing a foot inside Joel's front door, Willa's gaze moved between Joel and his sister. What a great relationship these two shared. "There's nothing to make up for, really. Leigh's been a doll. Besides, I only changed a diaper or two. Joel did the real work."

"Don't let her fool you," Joel said, hooking an arm around Willa's shoulders. "She changed at least three. Maybe four."

This time it was Willa who smacked him on the arm. Incorrigible man. "Actually," she said, as Joel rubbed at the imperceptible red spot left by her hand, "We divided the chores fairly evenly. Joel took care of Leigh and I took care of Shadow."

"Shadow?" Jennifer frowned. Her gaze moved slowly from Willa to Joel. Her voice was flat when she asked, "What's wrong with Shadow?"

Joel stared down his nose at his sister in a brotherly sort of I-told-you-so. "Other than being left to fend for himself?"

Jennifer only shook her head. "Good grief. What happened to Howie Jr.?"

"I haven't seen him to ask. Willa and I haven't been back that way since the rescue mission. But Shadow's in a doggy heaven over at Willa's kennel."

"Well, then I do owe you." Jennifer reached out, took hold of Willa's hand. "For Shadow's room and board if nothing else."

Willa could really grow to like Joel's sister. "Don't be silly. He wasn't here long enough to make a dent in the dog food. Besides, Leigh enjoyed the familiar face."

"What? Like my face isn't familiar enough?" Joel

playfully groused, pulling Willa closer and possessively into his side.

"I think it's the fangs." Willa reached up, lifted one corner of Joel's mouth with the tip of her finger. "Leigh's used to Shadow's not the better-to-eat-you-with variety."

Jennifer grew still, her gaze moving between Willa and Joel, her smile growing in proportion to the lights dancing in her eyes. "Well, I need to get home, see what all I left undone on my way out. You two obviously have better things to do than babysit. And Leigh here will be howling for a bottle soon."

"That's my girl." Joel tickled the baby's chin. "Can't ignore the call of those wild Wolfsley genes."

"This one's a Collins through and through, Wolf Man," Jennifer said, ragging on her brother and his love life as only a happily married sister could do. "You want a Wolfsley baby, you gotta do something about it."

"Uh-uh." Joel shook a finger in her direction. "Don't be goin' there, Jen or we'll be keeping that dog of yours hostage."

"Oh, shoot." Her matchmaking efforts came to a sudden stop and Jennifer glanced at her watch, then at Willa. "Would you mind if I come back tomorrow for Shadow? I have a ton of errands to run tonight and I'm afraid...oh, I wasn't thinking. You probably need the space—"

Willa held up one hand. "Tomorrow's fine. And I have plenty of room. In fact, my three boarders are due to check out in the morning, so the timing's perfect."

"He won't be in the way?"

Joel stepped forward then, took his sister by the shoulders and turned her toward the door. "Go home, Jennifer."

"But—"

"No buts. Here's Scout's bag," he added, grabbing the tote out of the playpen. "Unless you need the rest of this stuff tonight, don't worry about it. I'll help you load it tomorrow."

Jennifer stepped out onto the porch. "If you're sure."

"Why am I experiencing déjà vu here?" Joel followed her outside. "I swear you've got the hardest head."

"Wrong, Wolf Man." This time Jennifer's grin was pure devilment—just like her brother's. "Unlike Leigh, I'm pure Wolfsley."

Joel scowled. "And what's that supposed to mean?"

An innocent shrug and a wink to Willa and Jennifer replied. "Nothing. Just that we have a tendency to stare a gift horse in the mouth instead of jumping at the proposition."

Joel looked at Willa then. "And I'm sure this makes perfect sense to you, being that you're one of them."

"Them?" Willa and Jennifer chimed in unison. Even Leigh lifted her head from her mother's shoulder to give her uncle a fat pout.

"I give up. C'mon Jen." He followed his sister onto the porch, walked beside her out to the drive where she'd parked her minivan.

Willa accompanied the duo, but stayed a few steps behind, wondering exactly what it was that had clued Jennifer in to her brother's new liaison. Not that Willa was surprised by Jennifer's perceptiveness, especially considering the closeness these two shared.

She'd strapped Leigh safely into her car seat and now stood at the minivan's driver's-side door, talking in low tones to her brother who wasn't exactly comfortable with the topic of conversation. This Willa could tell by the way he rubbed a hand over the back of his neck and avoided meeting Jennifer's eyes.

Joel was certainly prickly when it came to relationships, but then, he had that in common with most men, Willa mused. Besides, their relationship was more an affair than a true romantic entanglement.

And that might be a bit difficult to explain to a sister who wanted to see her brother married with children. At the sound of Jennifer's laugh, Willa refocused and looked up in time to see the other woman buss Joel on the cheek.

Jennifer hurried forward then, giving Willa a huge sisterly hug. "Thank you so very much. I can't tell you how much I appreciate your help."

"You just did," Willa answered and meant it.

A wily female smile adorned Jennifer's mouth as she said, "I also can't tell you to make an honest man out of him. But I wouldn't mind a bit should you decide to tackle that particular project."

"What project would that be?" Joel asked.

"Nothing, Wolf Man. Not a thing. Bye y'all." Leaving Willa with a wink, Jennifer ran back across the yard with a backward wave.

"I like your sister," Willa said as the minivan backed out of the drive.

"I like her, too." He squeezed his fingers around Willa's nape, turned her back toward the house. "Now where were we?"

Warily, she glanced up, ignoring the hairs lifting along the back of her neck. "What do you mean, 'Where were we'? You were on your way to the sofa and *Monday Night Football* and I was off to feed the dogs."

"I have a better idea," Joel said as they climbed his front porch. The mood shifted, settling into a tension as edgy and sharp as anything that had cut the air between them the last few days. "Let's go to bed."

He backed her into the front door then, his mouth coming down on hers before Willa could get out an answer. By the time his taste had become her taste and he lifted his head, the only answer she wanted to give him was, "Yes. My bed."

"Lead the way, Darlin'. I'm all yours."

Desire hatched and sprouted, bursting forth with wings from the pit of her stomach, fluttering upward to stir her wildly beating heart as she did what he asked, taking his hand to lead the way. Having Leigh to consider, Willa had spent the past five nights with Joel, in his house, his bed.

It was important now, tonight, to bring him home. This was her sanctuary and she wanted to love him here, behind the sheer white panels draped over the black iron canopy bed, underneath the comforter of deep purple and golden threads, atop pillows in hues from lavender to lemon.

Within minutes of walking into her room he lay naked at her side, his injured leg beneath him and in no way an obstacle as he brought his body close to hers. She felt the warmth of his male flesh pressed hard to her belly, the heat from his chest bearing down on her breasts, the fever of his mouth searching out the secrets of hers, open and wanting and not a bit shy in letting her know.

Tongues mated and danced as Willa fed Joel's thirst, for he drank greedily, teasing and nipping with his lips and teeth, demanding she meet him as an equal in a kiss that curled her toes. Oh, the bliss of such a thorough seduction, she thought, working to push him onto his back, wanting to climb onto his body and take her fill.

But Joel would have none of that. He shook his head and pinned her to the plush pillows, moving his mouth to her breast, rolling her tight nipples over the flat of his tongue. And then he suckled, long, hard, with a gift for arousal that left her whimpering and whining and wet.

Her response was what he'd wanted, expect...no, had known he'd lure from her, the cocky wolf, grinning as if her body were his. But then his lids grew heavy, the green in his eyes became the green of fresh and new beginnings. And Willa groaned as he moved down the bed, moved his mouth between her legs.

His tongue dipped low and swirled high, circling her most tender flesh until it swelled unbearably, sucking the nub into his mouth and drawing hard, releasing, teasing with flicks from the tip and pressure from the flat of his tongue.

He repeated the process, kissing her thighs, the

skin of her belly, returning to the female flesh that had grown nearly too sensitive to touch. And then he penetrated with one finger, two fingers, easing the way with the moisture he'd drawn from deep within and that he'd left behind with his mouth.

Willa was one big spineless nerve when, finally, he guided her onto her side and slid back up the length of her body. He lifted her leg over his then and entered. Breathlessly, she shuddered, looking into his eyes as he began to rock against her, the pillows behind cushioning her back as his rhythm grew wild.

She couldn't get close enough, couldn't get her hands on him as she wanted to. She wanted to feel his body, all of his body, his thighs and his tight flat stomach and his firm backside. Her fingers fluttered over his skin until heightened need drove her to dig into his flesh and guide his thrusts.

She could feel him so deep, so thick, filling her so fully until she couldn't feel anything anymore. She was an explosion waiting to happen. A woman's heart wasn't meant to beat this hard, this fast. Her body wasn't meant to ride wave after wave without drowning in the man whose art was pleasure.

She cried out then bit down on his shoulder as release came in a gloriously heated explosion. She strained for every shudder, every shiver, straining until she was spent. And then Joel came, too, pouring into her body with the power of a man, taking her hard and forcing her deep into the pillows with the urgency of his completion.

Willa gave up to his strength then, allowing him the pleasure he sought and taking more pleasure than she knew possible by giving herself to a man.

Her heart swelled until the joy reached for her spirit, her soul, all the mental places that weren't supposed to be a part of their relationship.

All the places that were.

SUMMER BROUGHT Willa's heydays. Vacations staggered through the months of June, July and August guaranteed her kennels never wanted for boarders. Gordy patrolled the grounds like a member of campus security, reporting back when his canine instincts found anything amiss.

This year, June's heat seemed more oppressive than usual for a Texas Gulf Coast summer. Soaring temperatures sapped her strength and she was grateful for her border collie's sharp eye. He pulled his weight beyond his role as companion and she rewarded him nicely.

She rewarded Joel, too, for he was an awesome help. He'd gone back to work at the end of April— three weeks to the day after they'd become lovers. He'd surprised her by waiting that long, by not cutting off the cast himself and forging his own release papers. He'd been that antsy and impatient.

Once his cast had come off, he'd spent a lot of time in his home gym working to rebuild the muscle he'd lost. His weakness came as a surprise to the Wolf Man. It seemed he considered himself invincible. Being reminded of his human nature— that he could break as well as bend and that recovery came with time, not on command—made Joel a bit of a grump.

Now that he was mobile again, he had a month's worth of strength training he needed to show off. He didn't hesitate to hop through the shrubbery separating their yards any time he saw her working.

He took upon himself a few of the more arduous tasks, ones Willa had never had trouble managing before. This year, though, scrubbing down the kennels between boarders and hauling the fifty-pound bags of kibble and chow to the storage shed when the delivery service dropped the load on her driveway was more than she wanted to handle.

He'd even gotten into the habit of leashing up one of the larger dogs to accompany him on his daily run. That was probably the biggest help of all, because giving each of her boarders a daily dose of exercise was an amenity she prided herself on providing.

But in these long, hot and humid days of deep summer, exercise was the last thing on her mind. She got enough. Physical labor was built into her daily routine, and she certainly didn't lack for after-hours exertion.

The decision to become Joel's lover had been one of the best moves, the rightest moves, she'd made while navigating in the nebulous waters of male/female relationships. She'd never been more satisfied, more spoiled. More full and complete. She was also blessed with the certainty that Joel felt the same.

Physically, they were two halves of the same whole. And that cliché extended to their mental synchronicity as well.

They thought the same thoughts at the same time, finished thoughts the other started. They often spoke to one another without words, saying all they needed to say with looks and gestures.

It was almost frightening how well they meshed on those two levels. Especially when the third, emotional level was giving her fits. It shouldn't have, really.

She shouldn't have been surprised to find herself loving the man with whom she shared the best and worst of her days, the blissfully erotic hours of the night.

It was Joel who first came to mind when she had good news, or bad news, to tell. It was Joel's opinion she wanted when she considered raising her summer rates. It was Joel's input she asked for after interviewing three contractors who bid on replacing her roof. It was Joel's advice she sought when her minivan died and a vehicle purchase became priority number one.

Joel Wolfsley had become her best friend. Yet she couldn't share with him the thing she most wanted, most needed to share. The one thing a best friend, and this best friend in particular, deserved to be the first to know.

When she'd overslept that morning in mid-May and, even at Gordy's urgent bark, had had to force herself out of bed, she knew she was suffering from more than heat; knew she was ill-equipped to self-diagnose.

This lethargy wasn't going away on its own. It wasn't serious enough to be chronic fatigue, yet it was more than long hours working and too little sleep to recharge.

Her next thought had been of anemia. A very plausible possibility. Her diet wasn't exactly iron rich, but she'd never suffered such weariness before. And her periods had never been overly heavy—

A jolt of panic had scorched a wild path from her heart to the pit of her stomach. It was hysteria that had driven her from bed to bathroom and the dated record hung inside the medicine chest.

She'd flipped back through the pages, knocked the calendar into the sink, fished it out and kept from shaking long enough to open the damp accounting of her cycle.

She'd marked her start date in April, but May…nothing. And now it was the first of June. Oh, God. It was the first of June.

Joel had been gone for a week of training in the middle of last month. He'd asked about her timing just once before he left. She'd been due to start then and had told him so. But she'd never started.

She'd never started.

Of course she wasn't pregnant. One of her ovaries had been crushed in the accident. The Fallopian tube opposite had been cut. Cut, yes, but it hadn't been banded. And it hadn't been tied.

The doctors who'd treated her when she'd been a child weren't specialists but emergency physicians. Her family doctor, however, had concurred with the opinion that such extensive damage would preclude a pregnancy.

The gynecologist she'd been seeing for the past ten years had seen her records, but had never ordered up tests or suggested taking a look with an arthroscope at what eighteen years of healing time had accomplished. And he'd really had no reason to, not with such a dire diagnosis printed in bold black and white and no husband waiting in the wings.

So, when his nurse had taken Willa's blood that early June morning, and he'd come back with a wide smile and a big thumbs up, Willa had fainted. It seemed so silly now, fainting. But then she'd been both anemic and dizzy, and her head had been swimming and the shocking good news had unraveled her tenuous grip on consciousness.

After she'd come to, the miracle had coiled right back up into a tightly twined ball of nerves and trepidation. Joel was not going to be happy. He'd made his feelings on fatherhood clear. Neither was he open to the possibility of marriage.

Of course, trapping him into either had never been Willa's intent. Nor was it her intent now. Still, over the next week she found herself avoiding Joel and keeping her distance, and though he never came out and asked for an explanation, she knew he noticed her withdrawal.

When they slept together, long into the evenings after they had made love, he held her desperately close. He touched her often during the night as if seeking reassurance that she hadn't walked away and, more than anything, that he wasn't the cause of her withdrawal.

Even after he'd gone to sleep, she feared slipping from bed and waking him. And so she lay at his side and used her pillow to soak up silent tears.

She couldn't make herself tell her best friend, her best friend whom she loved beyond words or measure, that she was pregnant with his child. For once she did, nothing would ever be the same. He would no longer be her best friend.

And even the joy that filled her soul failed to soothe that sadness.

WILLA'S SADNESS didn't keep her from rejoicing. How could it? She was going to have a baby!

She wondered if she was carrying a boy or a girl, and she picked out names for both. To be fair, she should have asked for Joel's input, but she wasn't feeling very magnanimous these days.

She was eight weeks' pregnant. Her morning sickness was quickly quelled with a handful of crackers. She knew she was lucky in that her physical suffering was minimal.

But she was achy and bluesy and stupidly emotional and wanted to take it out on the man whose fault it was that she was swelling like a balloon—not a good idea since she still hadn't mentioned that the seed he'd planted had taken root.

She needed to tell him. She'd kept the secret too long already. The added stress of such intentional dishonesty was straining the bounds of their relationship. She'd grown snappish and cross and grew more snappish and cross when Joel questioned her moods.

She had to tell him. This baby was his, after all. He might not want to be a father, but nature and miracles had taken away his choice. Not long after the new year, a new baby Wolfsley would enter the world.

She was going to tell him. Then he could decide how much of a role he wished to play in his child's life. His decision would ultimately affect Willa's future, whether she stayed in the Houston area or left Texas to bring up her child alone.

Today. She would tell him. Today.

She whistled for Gordy. He loped across the yard. And not far behind loped Joel.

*Not just today, Willa. Now. Tell him now.* Easier said than done, she thought and sighed.

Why did he have to move across the lawn the way he moved in bed, with a purpose for every motion, a way of using his body that defined male beauty? Fluid movements emphasized the strength and symmetry of long arms and legs, the span of palm and breadth of shoulders, the pride in a head held high.

Why did her heart skip a clichéd beat when she looked up to see him? Why did her body tingle and heat? Why did she think of a hundred ways to greet him then trip over every word on her clumsy tongue?

Why did she have to love him? This man who would want no part of the gift he'd given her, who'd presented her with a legacy she'd never thought to claim. Why did it have to be the wolf she loved, the one determined to need no one, to walk through life alone?

Joel came to a stop, scrubbed a hand through Gordy's ruff then glanced up at Willa. His smile faded. His stance stiffened. His chin came up a defensive notch even as his brow went down.

Hands on his hips, he asked, "What's wrong."

Common sense and decorum never had a chance.

"I'm pregnant."

"YOU'RE PREGNANT."

They sat at her kitchen table, two adults, talking

rationally, calmly, over coffee. Or so anyone looking through the window on Willa's back door would think. Sure, there was a cup of coffee poured and waiting, but Joel, after a quick thrilling jolt that he didn't examine too closely, had long since left his chair to pace.

She was pregnant.

"How did it happen?" Lame statement, but true. "I don't understand."

She lifted one shoulder in a shrug that carried a belligerence he'd not seen before in Willa. "The usual way. Sex."

"Yeah. I got that part." They could've populated a town with the sex they'd had. He tunneled a hand through his hair. This might take a while. And more patience than he was sure he could hold on to. "You said you weren't able to have children."

"Doctors told me I couldn't get pregnant. God seems to have had a second opinion."

And the room fell silent.

Turning his back on Willa and her words, Joel braced his palms on the ledge of the sink and stared out the window above. He'd had a plan. That first day he'd walked through the academy's doors, he'd had a plan—for his future, for his life.

A plan that had just nosedived, taking his future and his life crashing down.

He'd been so cautious in all his previous encounters and so damn carelessly stupid with Willa. The only birth control method guaranteed 100 percent effective was abstinence.

How many street kids had heard him deliver that sermon? And had then suffered through his

refrain of *wrap that rascal?* So, why hadn't he prac-
ticed what he preached? Because he wanted to feel
her, skin to skin, without anything between.

At Willa's explanation he'd abdicated responsibility. Yes, they were both clean, but he still
should've worn a rubber. He didn't want children.
And he'd done nothing to prevent Willa's pregnancy. Stupid. Stupid. Stupid.

He hung his head, finished mentally beating
himself up then turned around. Arms crossed, he
leaned back against the counter's edge and
propped his weaker ankle over the other. Glancing
at Willa, he drew up short and frowned at what he
saw.

She sat in the straight-backed chair, her hands
laced on the table. Her ponytail was more severe
than usual and a noticeable slump to her shoulders
caught his eye. She'd appeared tired for a week or
so now and that hadn't escaped his attention, but
he'd chalked it up to summer heat and her go-go-
go schedule.

Why hadn't he noticed the changes in her body,
the body that he held close every night? The way
her hand trembled around the coffee mug she'd yet
to lift to her lips. The pallor to her skin. She hadn't
looked him in the eye since they'd come inside.
And that wasn't Willa.

After she'd made her announcement, they'd finished the evening feedings in silence, working as
the team they'd become. He'd noticed earlier the
smudges beneath her eyes. But now, even though
he saw her face from the side, he could tell the
color would not wash away.

He took a breath into his tight chest. "What did the doctor say? What happened?"

"The same thing that often happens to women who have their tubes cut instead of banded or tied. An eight-pound, five-ounce, twenty-one-inch 'oops.'" She slumped back in her chair. "All it takes is one good egg to fight its way through the scar tissue, jump the hurdle and set a downhill course."

He didn't know if she was bitter, defensive or scared out of her mind. Maybe she was a bit of all three.

Like him.

A long slow exhalation gave release to the building pressure. "I can't believe this. You had no idea?"

Hurt seized her expression with the impact of a fist to the gut. Joel felt it and flinched even as Willa schooled her features with a calmly resigned dignity.

"I've been through this with my doctor, Joel." She shook her head, pushing back loose strands of hair with one palm. It took a minute, but she seemed to settle at least a small piece of her conflict. She turned to face him.

Her posture straightened. Her chin lifted. "You have to know how foolish I feel. I should've learned more about my condition. Especially once I was old enough to understand. None of the mumbo-jumbo made sense at the time of the accident."

She took a deep breath, shuddered it out. "You can't imagine how frightened I was, listening to my parents and the doctors. I was hurt and confused and everyone around me was speaking in tongues."

This time her shrug signaled adult misgiving more than a child's alarm. "Maybe I didn't do the research because I didn't want to know. Maybe it was easier to live with the barren truth instead of holding on to some tiny spark of hope.

"I wouldn't have been able to stand that, counting down the days every month." Vehemently, she shook her head. "I accepted my fate. And I went on to live happily ever after."

"And now?" he asked quietly because he had no other words to say.

"Now?" She looked up at him and tears spilled from her eyes, trailing down her cheeks unrepentantly. "I'm going to have a baby, Joel. I'm going to be a mother."

She pressed her palms low on her belly and Joel swallowed the baseball-sized lump caught fast in the pocket of his throat. She'd gotten to her feet now and her face was radiant, a glowing porcelain that had him thinking of the picture of Jen when Leigh had been born.

The way his sister had looked in the hospital bed, holding that red-faced squalling wrinkled little thing and gazing into her new daughter's face like the miracle she held would change the world…Joel would never forget it.

He'd had to leave then—Jen's room had been filled with flowers and the pollen got to his nose in a bad way—but he'd seen enough before his eyes had watered up. And the way Willa looked now was Jen all over again. But better. Because for Willa the wonder was an honest-to-God-given miracle.

"A mother," she repeated and spun in a circle. On the toe of her work boots, she spun a circle. "I'm going to give birth and breastfeed and change diapers. I'll get to plan birthday parties and nurse broken bones and bite my fingernails over driver's education and struggle with homework and cheer at ballet lessons—"

"Only if it's a girl."

"What?" She returned from gazing into her future and focused on his face.

"No son of mine is taking ballet lessons. It's baseball or nothing."

Joel's comment settled between them, a heavy weight that dragged Willa's buoyant mood back to uncertainty and his to grim determination. She hadn't yet invited him to play a part in their child's life. No matter. He was prepared to acknowledge accountability and bear blame and get on with the adult decisions they needed to make.

He didn't need her invitation. He knew his position on this team. Fatherhood had not been part of his plans. But plans changed. The Wolfsley genes would live to see another generation and...

Ah, but life could be sweet. Joel almost busted a gut trying not to smile. Not only were the genes getting another run, so was the Wolfsley name. Four female Wolfsleys and not a baby named Wolf in the lot. His dad would break an arm patting himself—and Joel—on the back.

Unless Willa didn't plan to give the child Joel's name...

The cold water splash of reality hit hard and soaked his premature celebration. They had a lot to talk about and he didn't want to wait. Not when he had her here and he couldn't stop thinking that she might change her mind.

"We can negotiate on the ballet. I'm not that much of a sexist pig."

Willa shook her head, a tiny shake, a movement that barely moved. Her smile was equally slight. "That's okay. I have a feeling if this baby is a boy, the only interest he'll have in Swan Lake will be how many fish he can catch."

"That's a Wolfsley for you. A rod and a reel and nothing else matters." Joel took a big breath and a bigger step into the unknown. "This baby will be a Wolfsley, won't he, Willa? Or were you planning on him being a Darling?"

"I don't know, Joel." Returning to her seat, Willa pressed her laced fingers between her knees. "I haven't thought that far ahead."

It was a protective sort of withdrawal, Joel knew and understood. But he didn't know or understand enough. "How far along are you?"

"About two months."

"You've had tests?"

She nodded. "I saw the doctor last month."

Last month. She'd known for a month and was telling him now. His own mood shifted, leaving the arena of calm and rational to irritatingly grate against the grain. "Why'd you wait so long to tell me?"

"Honestly?" She looked up, her eyes wide and blue and totally open to his searching gaze. "I wanted this time for myself. To hold close all I was feeling. Just for a little while, you know?"

He didn't, but he nodded.

Willa went on, gesturing with her hands now as

if she could pluck the words she wanted to say from the room's tense air. "This thing that has happened, it's so incredibly precious. I didn't want to share it. With anyone. Not just yet.

"Not until I really believed I hadn't dreamed the whole thing. Or knew for certain that the doctor hadn't mixed up my test with that of another woman. A woman who still didn't know she was pregnant because I got her good news by mistake."

He couldn't imagine what she'd been going through, the doubt and disbelief, the wonder and worry. "You could've told me, Willa. I would've helped. With the doctor, at least."

"I couldn't. Not when I knew how you felt about having children." She hugged her arms across her stomach in a protective maternal embrace. "Not when there was a chance you wouldn't want me to have this child."

Joel couldn't respond. He had to think to breathe. Anger rose to the tip of his tongue and he had to bite down hard on the words to think clearly. *A chance he wouldn't want her to have this child?* Willa knew him better than that.

Or did she only know what he'd told her?

They'd been lovers for two months, two months of unbelievable sex that had him grinning like Sylvester with a mouth full of Tweety.

But just because he and Willa had spent less than a dozen nights apart since mid-April didn't mean she knew how he would react to her news—especially since they'd gone into this arrangement with a strict no-attachments policy.

She assumed the worst because he'd given her no reason to think differently. And, honestly? He hadn't known until hit in the face with those two words "I'm pregnant" how he'd react to such news. He couldn't say he was happy, no.

But he wasn't the one with the highest stake in this pregnancy. The decisions he had to make weren't going to come easy. Not when he'd been set on his course for so long.

He pushed away from the sink edge which had pressed a permanent crease into his hip and returned to his chair and his coffee. "Willa, listen to me. You're right that I don't want children. But you're wrong to think I wouldn't want you to have this baby.

"And I'm not going to turn my back on you or on our child." A deep breath and he said what he had to say. "I want this baby to be a Wolfsley."

Willa rocked in her chair, her gaze locked on his, working through an equation of thoughts until she reached an answer. "You want this baby to wear your name?"

Joel sniffed the air and warily nodded. He didn't like whatever was coming.

"You think that will make him a Wolfsley?" Her voice softened. "Will it, Joel? Is being a Wolfsley all about wearing the name?"

"Hell, no. That's not what I said." He flexed his fingers before he snapped the handle off his mug. No matter what trick Willa was trying to pull, this one was going his way. "He's already a Wolfsley. Nothing's gonna change that one gene-filled, sperm-donor fact."

"So, you're saying it's the name and the genes and the donated sperm that make a man?"

"Of course not. It's his honesty and integrity. His

values. His morals. The way he lives his life." He could play bad cop a hell of a lot better than she could. "Whether he runs out on a woman pregnant with his child, or stands by her side."

"Stands by her side. What does that mean, exactly?"

"Criminy, Willa. You want me to marry you? I'll marry you," Joel said and felt the earth swallow him whole. What the hell was he doing?

"No, Joel," Willa answered and Joel plunged deeper. "I don't want you to marry me. If you loved me, things would be different. But you don't. And *this* is how things are."

Teeth clenched, jaw aching, Joel stared and waited.

Willa stood, leaned forward, placing but a foot of room between their eyes. "If you want this child to be a Wolfsley, then you'd damn well better be there, ready to play your part in making him one."

---

## 10

---

JOEL HAD ASKED HER to marry him. She'd told him no—without a tremor in her voice or a moment of hesitation. It was amazing that the world—and Willa—had survived two such cataclysmic back-to-back events.

Adjusting to the darkness of the storage shed after the glare of the late June evening's six o'clock sun, Willa smiled to herself as her focus turned inward.

She hadn't forgotten a thing about that day three weeks ago when she'd informed Joel of her pregnancy. The memory sat on her stomach a lot better now than had the dose of confrontation she'd been forced to swallow then.

What a conversation they'd had that afternoon in her kitchen. She'd never thought he'd blow his top—that wasn't the way of the Big Bad Wolf. But still she had to give him credit. He'd taken the news a lot better than she'd expected considering the two-word bomb she'd dropped had literally exploded his life.

But that proposal. Willa shook her head, reaching for both feed pails stored on the shelf built into the shed's back wall. The look on Joel's face when he realized what he'd said.... She'd never seen any-

one try so hard to reach out and grab back words
already spoken.

For one fleeting moment, she'd thought that
startled expression might've signaled the shocking
revelation that, yes, he did love her. But that moment only lasted a heartbeat, during which her
mind switched gears from wishful thinking to
common sense.

Slamming and latching the shed's heavy slatted
door, Willa turned and squinted against the golden
glare. Dusting her hands together, she swallowed
thickly. No, Joel didn't love her.

Once she'd accepted that truth, she'd accepted a
second. Their relationship as lovers had reached its
end, sooner than expected but an end no less inevitable.

Placing her hands in the small of her back, she
stretched, amazed despite her emotional pain at
how great she felt physically. The end of her first
trimester had arrived, bringing the most amazing
difference in her energy level.

It was like the first, fussy weeks of pregnancy
hadn't happened at all. She couldn't remember
ever feeling so head-to-toe healthy. Lifting the two
pails she'd filled with chow, she followed the worn
path to the back of the kennels.

She was glad she'd raised her rates. Her ex-
penses hadn't increased disproportionately with
her summer business, but she was spending more
time working than ever before—and was determined to draw wages accordingly.

Soon she would have another mouth to feed and
she intended to fill her child's belly on her own.
The lone wolf could keep his money, his indepen-

dence and his future intact. He could also keep to his lair and out of her bed.

It wasn't that she didn't want him there. She loved him. Holding him close in those dark and quiet hours brought peace to her sleep and her dreams. And that precious connection of tangled arms and legs brought a contentment of heart she'd never known before Joel.

But since he hadn't spoken of feelings for her, pride and self-respect had become an issue. Their arrangement as lovers hadn't been based on such feelings. Instead, the bond of friendship and companionship and the power of physical attraction brought them close. Love, however, required more. More, it seemed, Joel couldn't give.

Since telling him of her pregnancy, their physical relationship had taken on a new intensity—and not only when they made love, which they didn't do as often these days. They still spent the nights together, most often at Willa's house, Joel slipping into bed long after she'd tucked herself in.

He held her close and touched her, but she was the one who turned in his arms to initiate intimacy. Each time she loved him, she gave up another piece of her heart. In return she was held in strong arms, stroked with broad hands, pulled back into a solid body and safely held. But that wasn't enough.

It was beautiful and it was tender and it was a lot to give up. Especially when she could've had it every night wearing Joel's name and his ring on her finger. But a ring and a name and a warm, willing, hard male body couldn't satisfy her most ardent, urgent desire.

She wanted to be Joel's love, not just his lover.

Gordy trotted up and sat at her feet, his tongue lolling and whining in that tone of voice that meant she had company. Not just company, but the one visitor guaranteed to put that doggy smile on that doggy face. The timing was right for Joel's shift to be over. But lately he didn't come calling until later in the day.

She decided he liked those hours best, picked them on purpose in fact, knowing that after a long day they'd both be too tired to talk about much more than the weather, the economy, politics— easy subjects that had nothing to do with their impending parenthood.

She still had a bit of trouble with that, investing in a partnership with a man who wasn't her partner. The only consensus they'd reached so far was that their child would be a Wolfsley.

For a man who hadn't wanted a child, Joel had been strangely adamant on that one issue, and Willa had done her best not to read anything into his insistence. Oh, she wanted nothing more than to give their child his father's name. But she'd meant what she'd said.

Being a Wolfsley had nothing to do with the letters that spelled out the name. And she'd needed reassurance from Joel that he understood the commitment involved, that he didn't plan to be a Disneyland daddy. That he'd be there for the not-so-fun stuff, too.

Right now he looked like fun stuff was the furthest thing from his mind, she mused, looking up to see him cutting through the hedge between their driveways. He wasn't moving as purposefully across her yard as she'd grown used to him doing.

His long-legged stride seemed almost hesitant in fact, definitely slow of pace, and Willa frowned.

Then she looked closer. Her brow relaxed, worry let go and hormones took charge. She blew out a long slow breath.

He hadn't changed before walking over and he did his uniform proud. More than proud, because the clothes he wore were more than a uniform. Dark navy pants, light blue short-sleeved shirt, badges, insignias, holstered weapon, dark framed, dark lensed sunglasses...

Willa's stomach did one flip then another until the tumbling of nerves turned into one long routine with each step that brought him closer. The setting sun bronzed his skin which already glowed with a midsummer tan. The hair on his forearms was bleached near white. The hair on his head was short but for the longer strands on top.

Willa allowed her appreciation to get personal, her imagination to peel away the external trappings. Joel Wolfsley had the body of a god, sculpted and toned and firmly muscled.

She knew what it felt like to run her hands across that wide chest, to taste the hair-dusted skin on his abdomen, to take him into her body and draw from him a response that left him a shuddering mess.

Right now, she was the shuddering mess.

Oh God, she was going to have this man's baby and she loved him with all her heart.

"You're early," she remarked and offered him a warm smile. It wasn't easy when her mouth was trembling and her eyes were threatening to spill tears of emotion.

His mouth quirked. "Early for what?"

She shrugged and opened the first kennel's wire-mesh door. "Early for you. Lately, it's been after dark before you show up 'round these here parts." She looked back at him over her shoulder. "You look good in the glasses, by the way. Very...*Bad Boys.*"

"Thanks. I think." He nodded toward her smaller feeding buckets. "You need help with those?"

"I'm fine. Strong as an ox. Uh, the female version anyway." She flexed her free arm and decided not to accept his help on principle. And because, now that he'd gotten closer, the frown lines across his forehead were noticeable and deep.

She'd been right in gauging his step as hesitant. "What's up?"

He came closer, out of the sun and into the kennel area shaded by an abundance of tall pines. "I came to deliver an invitation."

"From whom?"

"My mother."

*His mother?* Willa dropped her pail of Dog Chow. The tiny dachshund in the pen rushed to gobble the bounty. She grabbed him up, squatted to scoop the spill. "No you don't, Little Frank. Your bottomless pit has a bottom and it only takes a half cup of food to find it."

Dog in hand, she started out of the pen, stopped when Joel handed her the whisk broom he'd grabbed from the pegboard behind her awning-covered work bench. "Thanks. You read my mind."

He held the dustpan while she swept up the spill. "Part of the job, ma'am. All part of the job."

A job which was difficult to finish with the low-flying dog moving in and out and around their legs. Willa moved Little Frank and his food bowl to the rear of the pen and out of the way.

"Stay," she ordered and hoped for the best from the feisty pup. Joel had all but the far-scattered nuggets of chow off the floor when she returned to finish the job. "I'd say mind reading, not to mention kitchen detail, is a bit above and beyond the call of duty. Wouldn't you?"

"Depends on whose kitchen I'm detailing. Or whose mind I'm reading."

"That comes easy to you? Reading minds?" Latching the first pen, she moved to the second. Anything to delay discussing the invitation that brought him here.

Joel shrugged. "Some are easier than others. The minds with not a lot going on upstairs are easy to anticipate."

He held the bucket while Willa measured food into the bowl of the Airedale in the next pen. "And the rest?"

"Just as easy. Once you get beyond the smoke and mirrors."

Uh-oh. "Smoke and mirrors?"

He nodded. His sunglasses obscured his eyes. "Classic tricks. Like distraction. Avoidance."

Double uh-oh. "Avoidance?"

"Yep. Changing the subject's an old standby. Suspect thinks I'll lose track of what I'm after. Backfires as soon as I get a look at his eyes."

Willa backed out of the Airedale's pen, skipped the third and moved to the fourth where a large

Doberman sat waiting for his meal. "You might want to let me handle this one."

Joel's hand flattened against the wire-mesh door. "It's not working, Willa. The distractions. Or the avoidance. I don't have time to play games."

Willa closed her eyes, opened them slowly. "Fine. What is it exactly that I've been unable to distract you from?"

Funny how he looked so distracted when she said that. Like he *had* lost track of what it was he was after. It was the way he looked at her, and she couldn't even see his eyes—only his stance and set of jaw, the pulse in his throat and flush of skin.

He pulled his sunglasses from his face. "My mother's invitation."

"What sort of invitation?"

"Saturday. The annual Wolfsley Fourth of July Come 'N' Get It. You're invited."

Trepidation grew bolder but with steps slow and even, she carried the bucket of food to the work-bench and left it there. Then she turned her full attention on Joel who'd followed.

"Why am I invited?"

"She wants to meet the mother of my child."

"You told your mother?" Her voice barely reached a whisper, blocked, as it was, by a fast rising flood of anger.

"And my father. By now I doubt there's a Wolfsley who doesn't know."

Willa wasn't sure she could speak. She wasn't sure she could breathe. "How could you!"

Joel arched a brow. "How could I what?"

How could he sound so arrogantly cool? How

could he be so arrogantly presumptuous? How could he be so arrogantly…within his rights?

She gestured expansively, even as her fury washed away in near tears of resignation. "Tell everyone. How could you tell everyone?"

Joel reached for her, with one hand he lifted a strand of hair from her shoulder, tucked it behind her ear, slid his palm to her nape and said, "Willa, Baby. How could I not?"

He couldn't look at her that way. She couldn't stand it if he looked at her that way, his eyes so searching, so honest, asking her to see his side, to understand.

She couldn't stand here while he looked at her that way, not now, not when they hadn't first discussed who they would tell, how they would break the news. They had so much to talk over, to decide on, to plan for—all about the joint future they weren't going to share.

No, she couldn't bear for him to look at her. Not when her heart was breaking because she loved this man, the best friend she'd ever had, the lover she'd always wanted.

This man, who would never be her love.

He'd agreed to be part of their child's life. So, why was she surprised that he'd told his family? He might be a loner but he was a Wolfsley, part of a loyal pack. A pack that would welcome her child—and to which she would never belong.

She pulled away and began to pace, stopped, pushed her hair back from her face with shaking hands. She had to get a grip. And now.

"Okay. What exactly did you say?"

"I told them we got naked and made a baby.

Criminy, Willa. What do you think I said?" He looked away, looked back, braced both hands at his hips and sighed. "I told them we've been involved for a while now. In a relationship. And that we're going to have a baby."

*Think, Willa. Think.* "Did they ask? What type of relationship?"

"I think they figured that one out on their own." He frowned then, and stared at her as if he was looking at a stranger, or worse—a woman he wasn't sure he wanted to know. "Willa? Are you ashamed of what we have?"

The question's emotional punch struck with a solid blow, delivered as it was in a voice gone wooden, cold—so unlike Joel that Willa had to take a step back. *Now, Willa. Tell him now that it's over.*

"Ashamed? No, Joel. Not ashamed. But I'm not sure...that under the circumstances..." She studied her short fingernails, kicked a twig from the toe of her boot. "That maybe it's not wise to... continue. Now that things have...changed."

"Changed?"

She nodded. It had been hard enough to say what she'd said. She wasn't going to compound the hurt by saying more. Not when her knees were feeling the strain of keeping her upright.

"How have things changed, Willa? Because we're having a baby?"

"Friends being lovers is one thing. Friends having a baby puts a new twist on things, don't you think?" She backed into the workbench and crossed her arms. "There's more at stake here now than just a good time."

"We've always had more going for us than a good time, Willa," he said and she looked away.

Joel leaned closer, lowered his voice until his words reached deep into the part of her she was trying to keep in one piece.

"You know as well as I do that what we've done—" He moved forward. "What we've had—" He took another step. "This thing between us—" He was near enough now that he breathed Willa's breath. "It's not going to go away just because you want it to."

Because she wanted it to? Because she wanted it to? Even as his voice seeped into her pores like soft honey, his words grated over her skin. Pride could be a funny thing. Especially when an emotional connection she valued, a physical bond she cherished was made to sound like an...an...allergy.

Hackles raised, Willa lifted her chin and stood toe to toe with Joel. "Yes. We've had more than a good time. We've had a physical relationship rare even between committed couples. We've laughed and played and talked long into the night.

"Talked about things that matter, things that mean a lot. Things we haven't shared with others," she said and then she bit her tongue before she said any more.

"But that's not enough."

"No." She shook her head. Vehemently. "It's not. Not anymore."

"Because of the baby."

*Because I love you.* "Yes. Because of the baby. I guess I'm not quite as progressive as I'd thought." She relaxed a bit, even drew a steady breath. "When this relationship involved you and me and no one else, we only had ourselves to answer to. But now we have a child to consider."

"I want to be involved in our child's life, Willa. You know that." He blew out an exasperated breath. "Call me dense, but I don't see the problem."

It would be hard for him to see what he wasn't looking for. "Okay, then. I'll try to clear the fog. Say it's career day. First grade. Our child wants nothing more than to show off his Big Bad Wolf dad. All those badges. That big bad gun. You with me so far?"

Joel nodded. Looked tolerantly bored.

"Great." Willa began to pace, building up the steam to knock that bored façade into tomorrow. She could deal with anything but indifference. "Now, he tells his teacher he's not sure his father can make it. To career day. In fact, he hasn't seen his father since the last time he spent the night with his mother. He doesn't know when his father will show up again."

Joel shifted his weight from one foot to the other.

Willa went on, illustrating her points with one expressive hand. "'So, your parents don't live together?' his teacher will ask. And he'll tell her that, no, they don't. They're just real good friends. His father comes over when he can to help with homework and curve balls and to spend the night with his mother."

Joel looked off into the distance, looked back. "You make it sound worse than it is."

Willa stopped pacing, made sure she stopped in his direct line of vision. "No, Joel. I make it sound exactly like it is. Exactly. Like I said, we have a child to consider now. You and I may be perfectly comfortable with our...arrangement. But not all the world is so tolerant. And that's the world our innocent and impressionable child will encounter."

"Criminy, Willa. There're a lot of kids whose parents don't live in the same house."

"Do they sleep together?"

The tic in Joel's jaw jumped. The pulse in his temple flared. "I just don't know. I guess I'll have to take a poll and get back to you."

"You do that," she said, her voice incredibly even when everything inside her was upside down.

Joel spun on his heel, retreated six steps and stopped. Turned. Shoved his sunglasses back on his face. Looked at the ground then, mouth grim, at Willa. "About Saturday."

Willa nodded and reached for the bucket of chow. She could do this one thing. Just this one more thing. "Sure. I'll go."

"I'll pick you up at ten?"

She nodded again. And then she watched him walk away.

It was the hardest thing she could remember doing in her life.

THE WOLFSLEYS LIVED in The Woodlands, a community of executive homes hidden beneath acres of forest north of Houston. Street signs were ground level and billboards nonexistent.

Green belts cut through the wooded areas, allowing easy foot access to neighborhood schools and parks. To get back to nature, residents had only to open their own front doors.

The Wolfsley home sat deep in the corner where one road curved into another and had a backyard of at least half an acre. It made the perfect setting for a family cookout when the family was the size of this one. There had to be thirty people gathered around here.

"Don't worry," Joel said, placing a hand on Willa's shoulder as he walked beside her. "Not everyone here is a Wolfsley."

"I was beginning to wonder." She was beginning to have heart palpitations. The six-foot cedar gate latched behind them and Willa jumped.

Joel chuckled, squeezed her shoulder, moved his hand to the base of her neck. "Nervous?"

"Of course I'm nervous. I'm being thrown to the wolves, here." She pulled up short, dragged Joel to the side of the house where deep green shrubbery standing eight feet high hid them from the backyard party. A perfect place to make out, she thought, and wondered if he ever had.

"Tell me something," she said, pinching the bridge of her nose between forefinger and thumb. "Besides your parents, who knows about us?"

"About *us*?" Joel emphasized the last word just enough to make Willa squirm.

She'd turned down his proposal. She'd sent him packing. There was no *us*. "Okay. About the baby. Who knows?"

"Who in general? Or who out of the people here?"

Dread settled to the cold tips of her fingers. She leaned back against the brick wall of the house and closed her eyes. When she opened them again, Joel was leaning over her...and his eyes were smiling. Why were his eyes smiling?

He wore a sleeveless black T-shirt today with denim shorts and athletic shoes. One hand was at his waist. The other he'd braced on the wall above her head. He was way too close when she needed distance.

Here she was, doing her damnedest to be independent and strong in the face of the coming ordeal, and still she wanted nothing more than to feel those strong arms around her, to bury her face in his wide protective chest.

Love was stupid.

*Strong, Willa. Be strong.* "Everyone knows then?"

"Only the family."

"And how much of your family is here?"

"Well," he hedged. "That's hard to say."

"Try."

"Hmm. Annie's in school and waited too late to get a flight out. But I'm pretty sure she's the only one missing. Moira's here. Carolyn and her husband. Jen and Rob, of course. All the nieces and nephews and I think a couple of my dad's sisters and their families. The rest are neighbors and friends."

"So, half of the three dozen people here are family and they all know that you and me—me, a woman they've never met before—are going to have a baby." Eyes closed, she slumped against the wall. "Great. Just great."

"You don't know the Wolfsleys, Willa. Babies are a major event. This one more than usual."

She was afraid to ask, afraid to open her eyes—

especially once she'd let his tone sink in and realized even his voice was smiling. What was with all the smiling? For no reason she could put her finger on, he was making her insane on purpose, the devil.

Prying open only one eye, she repeated, "This one more than usual?"

"I wasn't having kids, remember?"

She nodded.

"So, this one means a huge celebration. Makes up for the big-time disappointment my folks felt when I chose career over family."

"Disappointment? In you?"

He shook his head. "Not in me. No. They supported my decision completely. But they were disappointed that the Wolfsley name would end with me. Now there's a chance it won't. If our child is a son."

"I feel like a specimen. On a slide. Under a microscope." She covered her face with both hands, peeked out at Joel from behind spread fingers. "Half of three dozen people, minus the one who waited too late to get a flight, have all come to see the woman who holds the Wolfsley future in her…womb."

Joel pulled her fingers away from her face, pressed them, entwined with his, to his chest. "No, Willa. They've come to see the woman who managed to capture the wolf."

*Capture the wolf?* She looked up. Her stomach plunged down. No. She couldn't have heard that right. "Wha—"

"Joel? Is that you hiding in the bushes? And why

*are* you hiding in the bushes?" A pause, then, "Maybe I should come back later?"

Joel threw back his head and laughed. "No, Mother. You don't have to come back later."

"All right. As long as you're certain."

"I'm sure," he said and released one of Willa's hands as his mother appeared. "Mother, this is Willa Darling. Willa, my mother, Madelyn Wolfsley."

Madelyn Wolfsley had Joel's green eyes in an attractively made-up face of classic features. Her short silver hair was sassy and stylish, her lithe frame equally smart in a sunshine-yellow camp shirt tucked into crisp khaki slacks.

Willa pulled in a deep breath, took Joel's mother's offered hand and, seeing the welcoming smile on the other woman's face, marginally relaxed. "My pleasure, Mrs. Wolfsley."

"Madelyn, please. And, Willa, dear, no. The pleasure is most definitely mine." She held Willa's hand firmly between her own. Her voice was Lauren Bacall rich and genuinely warm. "I know you must be feeling overwhelmed, facing this bunch all at once."

Overwhelmed barely covered what Willa was feeling. Over her head. Drowning. Buried alive. Any of those was closer to explaining her trouble with breathing.

"Actually, I didn't know until about five minutes ago that there'd be a bunch here for me to face."

Madelyn turned a mother's displeasure on her son and his lack of manners. One eyebrow arched in a falsely haughty reprimand. "You didn't tell her you were bringing her here to meet your family?"

Joel ran a hand over his short hair. "I didn't mention who all would be here, no."

Madelyn poked a finger into his shoulder. "You. Go find your father. Willa and I can get acquainted much better without you hanging around."

When Joel made no move to move, Madelyn gave an exasperated sigh, crossed her arms and tapped one loafer-clad foot. When he still refused to budge, she turned her request into a teasing attempt at intimidation. "Move it, Joel Scott Wolfsley, before I drag out the family albums."

Joel scowled playfully at his mother. "Is that a threat?"

"What do you think, Willa?" Madelyn tapped a finger to her chin. "Should we start with the bearskin rug pictures? Or maybe the bathtub shots?"

"Willa's seen me naked, Mother," Joel said before Willa could get a word out. "You'll have to do better than that."

"Joel!" Willa gasped. The man was totally incorrigible.

He raised a brow in Willa's direction. "Just making sure you know I'm not abandoning you. Or leaving under my own free will."

Willa glanced from Joel's solid six-foot-two to Madelyn's slender five-foot-eight. The battle lines were drawn. "I can see you're being steamrolled. So, you might as well go already. Don't let me stop you."

He glanced first at Willa then his mother. "Ya know, it's a cryin' shame when a man's run out of town on a rail by both his mother and his woman."

His woman? Willa's heart slammed against her ribs then settled into a wild rhythm. She searched Joel's eyes, found sparkling humor and a hint of a promise of...what was it?

Try as she might, she couldn't put a name to what it was she saw—because every name that came to mind contradicted what she knew of Joel's feelings.

But then she decided she didn't know a thing about his feelings because, before he walked away, before he heeded his mother's request, he dropped a kiss on the tip of Willa's nose.

What was he doing? Willa thought, watching that gorgeously broad retreating back. Joel wasn't so insensitive as to play with her heart.

And he had no need to put on a show for his mother. The innuendoes and flirtatious play didn't fit with the way he'd barely spoken to her since the showdown at the kennels.

What in the name of all her dogs was going on here?

She didn't have time to wonder further because Madelyn took hold of her hand. Willa sighed, turned and met the other woman's gaze.

Madelyn squeezed Willa's fingers. "You two throw off some mighty powerful vibes."

"Joel and I?"

A nod. A smile. "A blind man could see how much he loves you."

Loved her? Loved her? Willa shook her head. "Madelyn, no. You're wrong. He doesn't love me at all."

Madelyn's eyes widened, then narrowed, then gentled and misted over. "Oh, Willa. Darling. We need to talk."

# 11

"THAT'S SOME WOMAN my boy's got there." Fred Wolfsley joined the three men standing watch over the beef brisket and pork ribs smoking on the backyard pit. He'd made his way back across the yard after a private conversation with Willa that Joel had timed at twenty-four minutes. "Brains and beauty both to be reckoned with."

"And not a bad sense of humor to boot." Rob Collins raised his longneck in salute. "Bet she could give that wife of mine a run for her funny bone."

"You done good, Joel." Fred's brother-in-law, Don Karr, glanced up from mopping sauce across the slabs of ribs. "I talked to Willa a while ago about that ol' bluetick hound of mine. She's gonna board Scooter at a discount when me and Karen go to Vegas in September."

"She's a business woman, Don. You told her how often you and Karen travel. She'll spoil that dog until you have to board him with her every time." Fred inspected the meat then lowered the heavy pit cover. "A smart cookie that one, right, Joel?"

"Yeah. She is," Joel said automatically in answer to his dad. Truth and the obvious were like that. Automatic. He lifted his beer and left the rest of the conversation to his dad, his uncle and his brother-in-law, turning his attention to Willa.

He looked across the yard to where she stood talking to Jen. Earlier it had been Carolyn and before that Moira. His sisters had echoed his dad's, his uncle's and his brother-in-law's observations.

That was some woman he had there.

She'd traded her trademark work boots today for simple brown leather sandals. Her denim shorts were darker than his, shorter than his and her long, long legs a whole lot nicer to look at.

The plain white blouse she wore had the feel of an expensive handkerchief, soft and deceptively simple when, having seen four sisters shop over the years, he knew it cost a small fortune.

Her hair had regained the bounce and shine and unruly attitude he'd noticed missing in her early days of pregnancy. Her eyes shone as blue and as bright as the pansies in his mother's flower beds. Her smile came from the heart. He knew that. He'd missed that.

He'd missed her.

He'd known Willa was special that first long day and night they'd spent together. But he hadn't realized what he'd found in her until recently. And looking at her now…all he could do was drool. And grin. A grin that came a lot easier these days after all the thinking he'd been doing.

A guy tended to do a lot of thinking after learning he was going to be a father then being dumped by the woman carrying his child. That combination pretty much shot the wad of male emotions.

Joel had questioned everything lately, from what he felt for Willa, to what he felt about himself, to why he felt so strongly about his job. He'd weighed the cost of priorities against the value of compromise and then factored in the loss of his relationship with the mother of his child. The solution to the equation had not been easily reached.

He loved his job, being on the street. It took a certain personality to face what he faced day in and day out. To see the greasy underbelly of a city, the pit of inhumanity, filth in human form, predators dealing in flesh, drugs—any market where money came fast, came easy and came in amounts that made the lure of the dark side hard to resist.

He'd seen it all and was proud of his record. He'd served, he'd protected, he'd put away the scum. The job had never been easy, but he'd never had the added stress of taking it home to a family. He'd been able to unwind with a beer and the blues, bass fishing and barbecues. It was the way of the lone wolf and it had served him well.

Until Willa and their baby.

"Thanks." His dad's offer of a second beer brought him back to the present. But only for a moment. He tuned out most of the golf stories, the stock-market discussion, the political debate and watched Willa work the crowd.

He loved her. It was such an easy thing to do, though it had been a hell of a revelation to come to grips with.

Once he'd admitted to himself what exactly he felt, he had panicked. Love was not a part of his plans. He didn't know what to do. What choices to make, what changes to make, because both were inevitable if he and Willa were to have any sort of future.

He'd thought of a departmental transfer. He'd thought of a career change. Teaching criminal justice appealed and a return to school for the necessary certification wouldn't take a lot of doing. He'd still be in the business of serving and protecting by sharing his experience with others.

Thing was, he didn't know if he and Willa had a future. When he'd blurted out that bass-ackwards proposal, she'd rightfully accused him of not loving her. At the time, he'd been blown away by her news and couldn't respond.

He hadn't known what she'd wanted or expected from him. He hadn't had enough presence of mind to know what he expected of himself. The proposal had come out of nowhere, like a scripted line called for at that particular point in the plot. And he'd been relieved, so relieved, when she'd said no.

Later he'd been insulted, angry and finally confused enough to seek advice from his father. Who'd told his mother. Which meant he'd heard a parental talking-to the likes of which he hadn't heard since eighth grade.

Once punishment had been handed down in the form of cold ham sandwiches instead of his mother's fried chicken and mashed potatoes, he and his dad had talked. Really talked. About careers and families. About sacrifices and responsibilities. And even for a while about feelings.

Joel had left his parents' home that evening still hungry, but carrying a sense of accomplishment. He and his dad had made great headway on the engine. And he'd made a lot of progress making sense of the last few weeks.

Yeah. He loved her.

So, now what was he supposed to do about it?

"SHE WAS A DOLL, really. Weren't you, Sweetie?" Willa bounced Leigh on one hip while her mother brushed grass and mud from her half-brother's knees.

"No blood, Robbie. Sorry." Jen dropped a kiss to the nine-year-old's head. "Now, go tell those cousins of yours that you're the first baseman, not first base."

The towheaded boy, his recovery made miraculous by the lack of blood, scrambled over every lawn chair between the picnic area and the makeshift ballpark set up at the back of the yard.

"You make that look so easy," Willa said, amazed that Robbie's sobs had ceased immediately once Jennifer cleared away the dirt. "The way he was crying, I thought he'd never walk again."

Jennifer chuckled. "We have a rule. No blood, no broken bones, no crying. We've somehow managed to convince him that unless a bone is showing or he needs stitches, then he's not really hurt."

"I'll try to remember that," Willa said, handing a kamikaze-diving Leigh back to her mother.

Jen caught her daughter, then caught Willa in a big hug. "I can't believe you and Joel are going to have a baby." She stepped back then, her eyes a soft and dreamy blue. "I've been ragging on him for years that playing pool or softball or fishing with his buddies does not a personal life make. I should've had faith that the right woman would open his eyes."

Willa wasn't sure that what she and Joel had

constituted a personal life for either of them. She wasn't sure that Joel thought of her as the right woman, regardless of his earlier teasing remarks. The only thing she was sure of was that she shouldn't pry, but Jennifer had left her an opening too good to pass up.

She pulled back from the other woman's warm embrace. "You don't buy his logic? That he can't have a relationship because of his career?"

"Puh-lease." Jen scowled. "Joel's such a guy at times. He goes into his manly cave to work out his manly problems. Only this time he never came out. If a career is a reason not to have a relationship, then Rob and I wouldn't be together. Joel knows that."

Jen glanced across the yard toward the smoking pit where her husband and brother stood with her father and uncle, four cooks spoiling the broth. "My brother's put me back together more than once after Rob's flown out of the country and into the middle of nowhere on a moment's notice.

"I lie awake those nights, holding his pillow close, knowing I have no way of contacting him except through channels lined with red tape. No, it's not the relationship I'd've chosen for myself, but it's the one I live with. And I'd live with worse if I had to." She turned to Willa then, blinked back joyous tears. "I'd live with anything for Rob. And Joel knows how I feel."

Willa didn't know what to say. She waited for Jennifer to compose herself, wondering so many things about the members of this family who had been introduced into her life. The one thing she didn't wonder about at all, however, was the depth of feeling each member had for the others.

She'd seen that today. Every time she'd been pulled aside for a private conversation, she'd seen how much love flowed from one Wolfsley to the next. She knew without a doubt her child would be welcomed here into the heart of this family, knew also that, even apart from Joel, she would be welcome here as…what? A friend? An acquaintance? A distant relative more than a few times removed?

Jennifer shook off her mood with a small laugh that brought Willa back. Taking Willa's arm, Jen headed toward the back patio and beyond where a half-moon-shaped flower garden sprinkled bright summer colors across a quarter of the yard. Fire-red geraniums, a mix of yellow and blue pansies, orange-hued day lilies and white daisies danced in thick beds of green.

Jen stepped carefully along the flagstone path. "Joel's wanted to be a cop for as long as I can remember. He was a pain to live with before he hit his teens. He'd arrest us for leaving our bikes out or for playing down at the ditch after a flash flood when the water was cold and disgustingly dangerous. Talk about a tattletale."

Willa had grown up an only child. She didn't know about tattletales. Or about pain-in-the-butt brothers. But she'd been a tomboy with enough rough and rowdy know-it-all male friends to relate. "What happened when he hit his teens?"

"He didn't hide what he wanted to do, he just didn't advertise it as he had in the past." Jen moved to sit on an iron bench hidden beneath the drooping branches of a willow. Leigh stood on the seat beside her, pulling at a lone branch of low weeping leaves.

Patting the seat for Willa to join her, Jen went on. "He wasn't totally immune to peer pressure and knew he was caught in the adverse dynamics of teenagers and respect for authority."

"But he never changed his mind?"

"Joel? No way. He changed his attitude if anything," she said, rescuing a handful of willow leaves from Leigh's mouth. "Looking back, I think that's probably when the Big Bad Wolf was born. He grew serious. Studious. Even a little bit dangerous."

"Dangerous? Really?"

Jen quickly shook her head. "Not physically, though he didn't hesitate to defend himself, his ideals or any of us. It's just that knowing what he wanted as early as he did put an edge on his personality."

Willa knew that personality. She'd seen that edge. "He grew up too soon."

"Exactly. Kids who used to come around, didn't anymore. I think he enjoyed that loner reputation. By the time he finished college and graduated from the academy, he was living his own press."

"Then the Big Bad Wolf was all for show?"

"Oh, it was real enough. And living that way as long as he has made it easy for him to put his career first in his life. Especially after seeing so many cop marriages fail." Jen lifted Leigh down from the back of the bench she was using as a ladder. "Thing is, he forgot one very important fact."

"And what's that?" Willa asked, intrigued by this look into Joel's past.

"He forgot about the man who lives beneath the skin of that wolf. Joel Wolfsley would never let his career destroy a relationship. That's not the kind of man he is. He's a lot like our father. Honest and honorable. But he's more."

When Willa frowned, Jennifer laughed. "Don't you dare tell him I said this, but he's a very sensitive, tender man. He doesn't show that side of himself to many people. But I've seen it. And I know he would never choose his career over a woman he loves, no matter what nonsense he spouts about his calling to serve and protect."

Time to return Jennifer's honesty. Willa offered a weak but accepting smile. "He doesn't love me, you know."

"Excuse me?" Jennifer had incredulity—her wide-eyed look, her doubting tone down to an art.

"This pregnancy was an accident, if you can believe that of two intelligent adults in this day and age." Willa still had trouble believing it, but her disbelief stemmed from a place she wasn't yet ready to share with Joel's sister.

"It's a long story and best saved for another time. Suffice it to say that Joel and I were lovers in the most practical, purely sexual sense of the word."

"*Were* lovers?"

Willa nodded. "We're back to being friends. Better friends than before, obviously. And friends who have a real good reason to stay on speaking terms considering this…partnership we're involved in."

"Partnership." Jennifer nodded slowly, glanced

toward her brother then back. "Do you love him, Willa?"

*Did she love him?* Willa looked across the yard to Joel. She picked him out there in that group of men. But she couldn't tell if he was talking. Or listening. She couldn't tell much at all with her vision blurred by unshed tears.

She blinked, blew out a breath. "He asked me to marry him, you know. I told him no."

"Because you don't think he loves you."

"He doesn't."

"Uh, Willa, Sweetie. We need to talk."

WILLA WASN'T SURE if she'd ever find clear skies or if she'd be stuck forever in this cloud of confusion. She and Jennifer had talked until Leigh grew fussy and had to be fed.

Jennifer wanted Willa to come along and continue their conversation, but she'd declined. It was barely after noon and she was all talked out.

Sitting on the secluded bench, and watching the gathering from afar, she picked one of Madelyn's daisies, plucked one petal then another.

*He loves me. He loves me not.*

So far today she'd heard from Jennifer, Carolyn, Moira, Madelyn and Fred that Joel loved her. Of course, if she took any of the Wolfsleys at their word, she'd have to believe that Joel hung the moon and the stars as well.

Her visit with Jennifer had been the most enlightening—and offered the most hope that Joel's bark was worse than his bite. Not that she'd minded his bite in the least. But his bark about needing to remain free and unencumbered wasn't

going to be easy to live with—not after seeing the
Wolfsleys in action.

*He loves me. He loves me not.*

How hard would it be to be a part of something
she wasn't truly a part of? Oh, she'd be welcomed
with open arms as the mother of a Wolfsley. But
she'd be an outsider. Willa Grace Darling. Not
Willa Wolfsley.

She choked back the sudden sob that came from
nowhere to burn a path from her chest to her
throat. Willa Wolfsley. That was the first time she'd
paired her name with Joel's.

She hadn't done any schoolgirl scribblings or
carved their initials into the trunk of a tree. She'd
had no reason to. She knew upon becoming his
lover that they had no real future ahead.

*He loves me. He loves me not.*

It was time to get practical. To make decisions
that needed to be made in the best interest of her
and her child. Whether she and Joel would share
custody. Whether she would seek sole custody and
grant him visitation. Whether she would sell her
place and move the kennels to another part of
town. She could provide quite well for her child on
her own.

It was time to face facts. Loving Joel—living next
door and loving Joel was not going to be easy. She
knew she'd grow weak where he was concerned.
She knew she'd invite him into her bed. She knew
she'd sell her soul to lie with him, to love him even
when he loved her not in return. And that couldn't
happen.

*He loves me. He loves me not.*

He loves me not.

HE FOUND HER on the bench beneath the willow tree. She sat with her knees pulled to her chest, her heels tucked close to her body, her arms wrapped around her updrawn legs. Her chin rested in the *V* of her knees and her unbound hair fell over one shoulder.

She followed his approach with big blue eyes, eyes wide with emotion, but dry, not damp. At least she hadn't been sitting here crying. It was bad enough that she'd been sitting here alone.

When he moved to sit beside her, she straightened, lowered her feet to the ground. Hands gripping the edge of the bench, she stared out into the yard at the women circling the long tables of food, at the teams of five playing softball at the back of the yard, at the group of men gathered near the pit while the meat was lifted onto platters and trays.

He wondered what she saw besides the boisterous preparations of family and food. She didn't share his memories of past Wolfsley gatherings. She didn't have his connection to the people present. She observed as would any outsider. Which was what she was. Even while she carried a child that wouldn't be.

He wondered how that made her feel.

He wondered how lonely her life had been.

He wondered if she knew how much he loved her.

"Willa. We need to talk."

WILLA LAUGHED to herself. She'd heard those words already from so many people that hearing it from Joel didn't come as a surprise. Talking seemed to be the Wolfsley way. "You won't believe how many people have said that to me today."

"Yeah? Well, we're a talkative bunch." Elbows braced on wide-spread knees, he laced his fingers together and leaned his weight forward.

Talkative. Curious. Well-meaning. Protective of their own. "Talkative." She nodded, glanced in his direction. "I guess you could say that. Y'all are a nice bunch, no matter. It's been fun meeting everyone," she said, but knew she hadn't sounded terribly convincing.

"We're just people, Willa. Maybe a bit rowdy. Definitely a bit loud. But just people."

People who belonged to one of the closest and craziest families she'd met in her life. Willa smiled—convincingly—and glanced from the wide backyard of goings-on to the man at her side. "Not just people, Joel. Family. You're lucky to have them. All of them."

"Except for when they can't keep their collective noses out of our business, you mean," he said without a hint of rancor.

The collective Wolfsleys had obviously been working on him as well today. And now that she and Joel were sitting here, together, in a spot secluded but not invisible to prying eyes...Willa groaned.

"You okay?" Joel reached over, squeezed her knee.

"I'm fine." She ignored the tender warmth of his hand and slanted him a sly glance. "You know what they're all thinking, don't you?"

Joel frowned, then looked out at the various faces sneaking not-so-covert glances toward the weeping willow. He rolled his eyes. "I can pretty much guess."

"So, do we sit here a while and drive them crazy? Make them wonder what we're talking about?" It was much easier to keep the conversation light and impersonal. The heavy stuff would come up soon enough.

"We can do that." Joel leaned back. He squared an ankle on the opposite knee, stretched his arms along the back of the bench, tickled his fingertips beneath the hair at her nape. "Or we can give them what they're waiting for."

Willa's head whipped toward Joel almost before the words left his mouth—and left in a voice gone as rich as the colors swirling around her feet.

What she saw in his eyes was not what she wanted to see in his eyes because nothing about that look was light and impersonal. It was dark and it was deep and it spoke of a change in the air.

Oh, God. She needed to keep him distracted. Keep the mood light. "You want to put on a show for their benefit?"

Joel sat forward again, leaned heavily on his elbows then shifted to the side to face her, his mouth a thin line, his throat working, his jaw set and firm. He lifted his gaze then, and his eyes, oh his eyes. They were green and they were feeling and they reflected all her dreams.

"No, Willa," he said quietly. "Not for their benefit. Not for their benefit at all."

No. Oh, no. Heavy had arrived and she wasn't prepared. Willa got to her feet before Joel had a chance to drop to one knee. Not that he was about to…she didn't know what he was thinking.

She only knew that the way he was looking at her was a look too intimate for a backyard party. It was a look that belonged in a bedroom, beneath dim lights and sun-dried sheets. A look that had her body responding with a flush of skin and a rapid pulse and a belly that fluttered with female need.

She'd thought at first he'd meant to kiss her, a playful teasing kiss for show. But he'd grown so somber and she couldn't deal with anything somber here and now with three dozen minus one people looking on and wondering. She began to pace. The path in front of the bench was short, but still she paced.

Slowly Joel stood. "Willa? What's wrong?"

She pressed her hand to her forehead. Of course he hadn't meant to propose. How silly of her. How totally ridiculous she was to think such a thing. How insane she had to be to torture herself this way, to stay here and stay calm and stay in one piece.

"Willa?" He took hold of her upper arm, gently squeezed. "What's going on?"

"I was just thinking—" What? What was she thinking? She caught a whiff of mesquite smoke and said, "It must be time to eat?"

"Getting close, I'm sure." Joel let go of her arm but stayed where he was, cutting her off midpace. "If food is really what's on your mind."

"No. It's not." She couldn't move so she sat. And she sighed. And she set her mind to putting closure to this conversation—a prelude for another closure to come later. "But right now it's all I can deal with. Please try to understand. As much as I'm enjoying myself, this isn't easy for me."

"Willa." Joel settled back at her side. His knee brushed hers and he left it there. "I didn't mean to make you uncomfortable by bringing you here. I just wanted you to meet everyone."

"And for everyone to meet me. Since I'll be giving birth to a Wolfsley." Funny how the truth sounded just as bad spoken as when it had been only an unvoiced thought.

Joel looked more than uncomfortable, but not quite guilty. He seemed to be searching, struggling as if this moment and these words would stop time if not well spoken.

"I didn't bring you here on a test drive, Willa. I'm not looking to see how well you fit in with my family. Or how they take to you. I wanted you to meet them and vice versa. That's all."

"It doesn't feel like that's all. It feels like I'm here on approval. That you're showing me off as a womb—not a woman." He started to speak and she cut him off with a wave of one hand. "Don't get me wrong. Everyone has been wonderfully warm and welcoming.

"But then I'll look up and catch you staring and I almost feel like you're grading me on some test. I'm not sure I'm passing." She closed her eyes, hung her head, lifted her lashes slowly. The gravel path beneath her feet seemed to swim. "I'm not sure I want to pass."

"Criminy, Willa. What're you talking about?"

"I can't do this, Joel. I can't exchange pleasantries with these people over and over again like I belong...when I don't."

"Of course you belong. You're carrying my child which makes you—"

"What?" She looked up sharply. Let him see her tears, she no longer cared to hide. "A family friend? That's not quite accurate, is it? You and I are friends. I suppose. But I'm not friends with the rest of your family."

Joel drew both hands over his eyes and down his face. "You just met them, Willa. Friendship takes time."

"And how often will I be seeing them? Holidays? There aren't a lot of those during the year, you know. What? Maybe a dozen? One a month?" She did the math and nodded. "Twelve hours a month is hardly enough time to nurture a friendship.

"Certainly not to the point where I see myself shopping for baby things with your mother. Or shopping for girl things with Jennifer. You know, the things girlfriends do."

Joel frowned. "Why not?"

"What do I have in common with either of them but you and this baby?"

"That's not reason enough?"

Her voice had grown shrill with her last question. She tempered it now. "If things were different, it might be."

"Different? What things?"

Was the man really so dense? "You, Joel. You. Now that you've reconciled yourself to the idea of parenthood, what's to stop you from changing your mind about other things? What if you fall in love and get married and have other children? Where am I going to fit in then?"

The change in his expression was that of an unexpected ice-water bath. But that quickly warmed into one of hot apple crisp and cream. He was entirely too pleased with himself for Willa's comfort.

He almost had to bite his own lip to hold back a smile. "That would bother you? If I were to get married?"

Dense wasn't the word she'd been looking for. Calculating, devious. Designing, sly. She got to her feet to pace again. "Never mind. Just never mind."

"Uh-uh. No way are you going to never mind your way out of this one. I want to know why what happens in my life makes a difference to your relationship with my family."

"C'mon, Joel. I can't bring our child here for the next Fourth of July Come 'N' Get It if you're here with a wife and new baby."

"Why not, Willa?" He was on his feet now, too. And in her way again. Taking hold of both her shoulders and managing only the gentlest of shakes. "Why not?"

"Damn you, Joel Wolfsley. I love you," she cried. And then she sobbed one loud hiccup and caught her breath. Great. Just great. Pushing her hair back from her face, she grimaced. "There. Are you happy? Is that what you wanted to hear? I love you," she repeated, her voice softer the second time around.

It was a moment before he spoke. A moment filled with his loud silence. Then his shoulders seemed to broaden, his chest grew full and wide, he seemed ten inches taller than he had moments ago and his smile encompassed all outdoors.

"Yes, Willa. It was exactly what I wanted to hear."

"Let's eat!" Fred Wolfsley's voice boomed across the yard.

"What timing, huh?" Willa sniffed. "Now you're off the hook. You don't have to say something you don't mean just to make me feel better. In fact," she turned to go, spoke over her shoulder. "You don't have to say anything at all."

He stopped her with a hand at her elbow and pulled her back. "Willa, wait. I don't say what I don't mean. You know me well enough to know that."

"Joel, I'm hungry. I'm eating for two, you know. And I'd like to go do just that."

He scraped a hand over his hair, his smile still there but fading as his tongue tripped over a dozen words before he said, "I need to say something here."

"No. Not here. Not now. Later." *Later when I won't have to put on a benefit show. When I can have my*

*heart broken in private just in case the news is bad.*
"Later. Okay?"

He nodded, and then she turned away before her pride and common sense succumbed to the desperate hope she felt when she looked in his eyes.

She could do this, this one thing, this one little thing, if she didn't have to look into his eyes.

JOEL HADN'T TASTED a thing he'd eaten. Oh, there were enough bare bones and puddles of barbecue sauce on his plate to account for the urge to unbutton his shorts and relieve the pressure on his stomach. But his mouth felt as dry and metallic as a spent shell. Must've been the empty taste left by the words he had yet to say.

He slumped back in his lounger, planted his feet on the grassy ground on either side and propped his plate on the seat between his knees. Even finishing off a second tumbler of iced tea didn't wet his whistle, and he needed it wet because he had a lot of talking to do.

The meal had been a necessary evil. He'd brought Willa here to meet his family, to get her away from the kennels for a while, but most of all to talk, to tell her of the things he'd been thinking, the conclusions he'd drawn, the decisions he'd reached. He'd have been happy to skip the meal altogether, but no one skipped meals around Fred and Madelyn Wolfsley and lived to tell the tale.

Listening to the men around him debate the future of Houston's professional sports teams, Joel glanced across the yard. Willa's lawn chair sat between Moira's and Jen's in the half circle the women had formed. Female laughter reached Joel's ears. Not Willa's laughter, but that of his sisters, his mother and the rest.

Willa had picked at her food, eaten a slice or two of brisket and half an ear of corn on the cob, but no more than a bite of potato salad or two of the baked beans. She hadn't touched the relish tray—not even for one of his mother's homemade pickles.

Pickles and pregnancy were a myth, he knew, or at least he thought he knew. Thing was, he didn't know nearly all he wanted to know—not about pickles and myths and old wives' tales and pregnancy in general, but about Willa. And this pregnancy. Their pregnancy.

He wanted to know if she did have food cravings and what she most wanted to eat. He wanted to know if she felt the baby move yet. How soon did that happen anyway? And when would he be able to feel the tiny kicks and jabs as their child grew in Willa's womb? Was she taking care of herself, following doctor's orders, getting enough rest, remembering her vitamins?

She laughed then and brought Joel back from the picture of her heavy with child. His child. Their child. He blinked hard, suddenly filled with the tenderest and fiercest need to hold this woman, to feel her heart beat with the life she so fully lived, with the love she so freely gave. Her life, her love, both of which had touched him and given his future a new direction.

He wanted her to share the rest of his days.

She'd finished eating now and stood to gather empty plates from the others in her circle. Leaning down, she spoke to his mother. Her voice was so sweet to his ears. He didn't know when he'd last heard it like that, pure and honest, sincere and unaffected. It was the voice of a woman who loved him.

She loved him and the world hadn't stopped. His heart had, but just for a moment. She'd said those three words and instead of seeing the end to his way of life, he'd seen a new beginning.

He'd respected Willa's obvious wish to wait and conduct their private business privately. But now that they'd contributed to the social niceties and familial harmony, they could make like a banana and split. He didn't want to wait any longer to get started on the rest of their life.

"Excuse me," he said to whoever remained in the group where he sat. He heard his dad's voice and Rob's but he wasn't sure if they answered or were only making more sports talk. His concentration was all for Willa.

He caught up with her at the end of the long tables of food. She tossed soda cans into the recycling bin, paper plates into the trash then turned and plowed into his chest with a loud, "Oomph."

"Joel. Sorry." A quick laugh. "Teach me to eat my weight in barbecue. The reflexes are bogged down in at least a gallon of sauce."

"A half ounce would be an exaggeration." He leaned over her to toss away his own trash.

She raised that imperious Willa brow. "You watched me eat?"

"Yep." He nodded. "And I'm afraid I'm going to have to place you under arrest."

"What?"

He took her upper arm and directed her toward

the gate at the side of the yard. "You can't eat like that and get away with it around here. That's a violation of statute 107.5."

"I'm under arrest for violating a radio station's call signal?" She hurried her steps to match his long urgent stride.

For it had become urgent, this mission he had to accomplish today. "Nice try, but I'm in no mood to cut you any slack. Now, let's go."

This was an anticipation he hadn't felt since... when? Childhood? Birthday surprises and Christmas had brought a sort of expectant thrill. But this was more along the line of the anxiety of waiting on report cards, SAT scores, college acceptance letters. The knowledge that no matter how certain good news seemed, there was always that chance of failure and rejection.

Shaking off as much of the sensation as he could, Joel pushed open the gate, propelling Willa through with his hand still gripping her upper arm. His truck was parked at the end of the long drive and he headed toward it.

"You know," she began. "You could've given me a chance to say goodbye. I'm sure your family thinks I'm extremely rude."

"No. They just think you're powerless to resist me."

"Oh, is that what it is?"

At least she hadn't contradicted him. That had to be worth a point in his favor. "Hey, they drew their own conclusions. I didn't say a word."

"You of the talkative bunch? Didn't state a persuasive argument in your own favor? I find that hard to believe."

They'd reached the truck now and Joel pulled open the passenger's-side door. Her lips a twist of a smile, Willa stopped and faced him, as if braced to outwit his next line of banter.

Instead of delivering words, he delivered a kiss to her waiting mouth. It was a kiss from the heart, not from the loins. A kiss of desire that encompassed body and soul. A kiss that was full and openmouthed yet gently tender and resonant with love. She tasted like the rest of his life and that was good.

He broke away then while he still could, and, before she could think of a comeback, he placed his hands on her waist and lifted her up onto the seat.

"What was that for?" she asked.

He wanted to tell her. Right here. Right now. He needed to tell her, had to tell her. But he couldn't. Not when the next minute might bring an interruption from the backyard, a neighborly neighbor or a drive-by audience.

They were parked at the very end of the driveway, after all, and this conversation wasn't for public viewing. He looked up as another car turned onto the street. "Let's get out of here."

Willa growled a loud, "Argh," as he slammed her door. "You're making me crazy," she added after he'd climbed behind the wheel.

"That makes two of us." He started the engine, glanced in his rearview mirror, shifted back up into Park. "Criminy. Robbie's bike's hanging from the tailgate."

"I'll get it," Willa said and was out of the truck before he could do the honors. He figured she had about as much nervous energy as he did and didn't want to sit and wait when she could move the bike herself.

He watched in the rearview mirror as she lifted the front wheel over the tailgate, bounced the bike on the ground, waited for the oncoming car to pass—

The car slowed, Willa leaned down to speak to the driver through the open passenger window. Then... What the hell? She opened the door and stepped closer, frowning toward the driver, shaking her head, glancing back at Joel whose senses were now on high alert. Hackles chilled the back of his neck with the cold reality of danger.

He reached for the door handle and was out of the truck just as a hand reached for Willa and jerked her down on the front seat of the car. The driver hit the gas and the open passenger door slammed into the back end of Joel's truck.

Joel bounded forward, stopped after one step when he saw the driver's face—and his gun. The Knight. The drug-lord scum Joel had taken down. And he had Willa.

The chill spread. Ice coated his spine with the cold of a fear he'd never known. Even the rage, the howling deadly rage that rose from the soul of the wolf failed to dispel the rabidly frigid crust of fear. The scum was dead meat.

Joel jumped back into the truck, slammed into Reverse, shot back out of the driveway and over Robbie's bike, then blasted forward. The car was but a hundred feet ahead when he reached into the truck's glove compartment for his gun.

He couldn't get a clear shot. Damn. He could see both the driver's head and Willa's but he couldn't risk shooting blindly into the car, or at the car, not with the way it was weaving wildly from one side of the road, where it bounced off the curb, to the other, scraping the first in a trio of parked cars.

Helplessness fueled Joel's fright and rage, and he jammed his accelerator to the floor. Please, God. Not Willa. This wasn't going to happen to Willa. She wasn't going to be used as revenge against him. Not as long as he could draw a breath.

The car ahead braked hard on screeching tires and in the worst of Joel's nightmares, Willa's door flew open. She tumbled from the car. His heart screamed. But within half a second he saw the tucked control to her dive and roll. *Make the choice, Joel. Willa or The Knight.*

No contest.

Joel slid his truck to a stop, shoved open his door and leaped out to run toward Willa. He never made it past the back end of his truck. The car hurled forward, The Knight whipped his head in search of his hostage, futilely reaching for the open door. He never saw the van parked in the street. He plowed into the rear quarter panel, his head lashed forward into the windshield then back.

Joel glanced over the truck bed to where she was up on all fours, dazed but with no visible injury. She waved him on. Pride surged from his deepest core. He'd chosen his she-wolf well. He moved back to his open door, reached behind his seat for his bulletproof vest and threw it in her direction.

Turning to The Knight's car, Joel saw him stumble out, gun in hand, blood streaming from a gash above his nose. The dealer squinted, took aim and fired. Joel dove into the truck as the shot ripped through metal. He cocked his weapon, took a deep breath and squirreled around to peer out over the hinge of the open door.

The Knight lurched drunkenly, got off another wild shot as Joel took aim. Tit for tat, he thought, wanting to wipe the face of the earth clean of this scum. But knowing his testimony would put away more of his kind, Joel pulled the trigger once, twice. The Knight went down, clutched his leg with his good hand, his shooting hand limp against the pavement. Joel rushed forward even while the other man strained to lift the gun.

The gun was up, inches off the ground, The Knight's hand shaking, his finger squeezing. Joel kicked out as the shot went off, and a burning trail of fire seared the top of his foot before the gun went sailing across the pavement.

Joel glared down, his gun trained down on the shooter as the skin on his foot blistered and pain took hold. "You're just damned determined that I'm not going to walk, aren't you? Well, guess what? My determination's a hell of a lot stronger than yours."

Joel stared down into stony silence and soulless eyes devoid of all but black-as-night hatred. He leveled his gun toward the center of The Knight's fetally drawn body. This man had nearly cost Joel the most valuable thing he'd ever known. Suddenly the dealer's testimony didn't seem so important.

The downed drug lord spat at Joel. "Go to hell."

Joel sneered and aimed. "You first."

"Joel! No!"

Willa's cry pulled him back from insanity to the

moment. He caught a peripheral glimpse of her moving toward him. "Stay by the truck, Willa. Don't come any closer."

Front doors were opening then, curtains pushed aside as the curious peered out. In the space of one second, Joel turned to have someone call 911. In the space of the next, three cars from two law agencies roared around the corner.

Within minutes the street was teeming with onlookers and crime scene chaos ensued. Joel surrendered the situation and gave his story to the responding officers, all the while watching the paramedics tend to Willa's cuts and scrapes until he'd had enough.

"I'll be back," he told the officers and, leaving them to deal with the human mess on the ground, limped toward his truck. He waved off the paramedics intent on tending to his injury. His focus was onefold and wouldn't wait any longer.

Wrapped in a light blanket designed to ward off shock, Willa sat sideways behind the wheel of his truck. Her eyes were bright in a face gone pale, yet her smile never wavered and grew wider as she watched him approach. At least until she noticed his limp and the shoe he'd lost to The Knight's last bullet.

"You need to get that looked at." Her voice was steady, but quiet. As loud as things were around them, he had no trouble hearing her.

"You okay?" he asked. She nodded but it wasn't good enough so he pressed. "You sure? Nothing's broken? The baby's safe?"

"The baby is well protected. And I didn't even break a nail. Not that I have any to break." She looked down at her long, strong fingers, her short practical nails.

Relief warmed him and he smiled down at his woman. He wanted to wrap her in his arms and take her away, to jump behind the wheel and leave this craziness behind. But she was right. He needed to have his foot looked at.

He took hold of her hands, both hands, squeezed her fingers until she looked at his face. Tears brimmed in her eyes, whether from the emotional impact of the moment or from a different source he didn't know. He only knew what he had to do, what he'd waited too long to do already.

He took a deep breath and said, "You have the right to remain silent."

"What?"

"Of course, I'd rather hear you say 'I love you.'"

"Oh, Joel. I love you," she said and this time he knew the source of her tears.

He felt like releasing a few of his own. "Good. You have the right to an attorney. If you cannot afford an attorney, one will be appointed for you. Or, if you prefer, we can go straight to the judge."

"The judge?"

"Or a preacher. Whoever can marry us the fastest."

"Marry us?"

"We're having a baby, Willa—"

"Which is no reason to get married."

He thought differently, but wasn't going to argue that point. Not when he had another. "You love me, Willa. You've said so yourself. More than once." He knew that because he'd counted.

"That's still no reason to get married," she said,

but he saw hope blossom. "Us having a baby and me loving you is just not enough."

"A lot of couples have less."

"But I need more."

"I know you do. So I want you to listen to me while I still have the strength to talk." Standing now on one foot, and leaning his shoulder into the frame of the truck, he placed his palms gently on either side of her face.

"I love you, Willa. I want you to be my wife. You're a good woman and you deserve better than the danger I've put you in. But I'll do my best to serve and protect you."

"Protect me?"

"With my life," he said and meant it.

"And serve me?

"Anything."

Joy was bright in her eyes, loving eyes, teasing eyes, eyes that made bachelorhood a bore and life with Willa an adventure.

"I accept. But I do have one condition."

"Name it," he said, ready to give her the world.

"It's about those handcuffs…"

# Epilogue

"CAN'T YOU GUYS move this bucket any faster?" Sirens blared overhead, lights flashed in through the ambulance windows.

"Hospital's ten minutes ahead, Wolf Man. We'll be there in plenty of time." D. Luza, the ambulance driver, had an ear to ear grin on his face.

Joel ground his teeth to keep from smacking it off the cheery guy. But then Willa groaned and squeezed the living daylights out of his hand. "We're almost there, Baby. Hang on, we're almost there."

"We're not going to make it." She panted, scrunched up her face. "I can't wait ten minutes."

H. Boone, the paramedic, met Joel's panicked expression. "She's right. This baby's got a streak of his daddy's impatience."

"Criminy. Not in the ambulance?" Joel looked from the medic to Willa—whose eyes were screwed shut, mouth a twisted grimace.

"Okay, Mrs. Wolf Man. Let's do it." The medic positioned himself between Willa's legs. "Detective? Get up there and support her back so she can push."

Joel did and Willa did and, three long pushes later, the baby did, sliding into the medic's waiting hands. Willa gasped and laughed. Joel gasped then loudly whooped. The medic only smiled.

"It's a boy," said the medic.

"It's a Wolfsley," said Willa.

"It's our baby," said Joel, tears filling his eyes.

And leaned down to kiss his wife.

If you enjoyed what you just read,
then we've got an offer you can't resist!

# Take 2 bestselling love stories FREE!

# Plus get a FREE surprise gift!

# Every Man Has His Price!

# HEART OF THE WEST

## At the heart of the West there are a dozen rugged bachelors—up for auction!

This August 1999, look for *Courting Callie*

## by Lynn Erickson

If Mase Lebow testifies at a high-profile trial, he knows his six-year-old son, Joey, will pay. Mase decides to hide his son at Callie Thorpe's ranch, out of harm's way. Callie, of course, has no idea why Joey is really there, and falling in love with his tight-lipped father is a definite inconvenience.

**Each book features a sexy new bachelor up for grabs—and a woman determined to rope him in!**

*Available August 1999 at your favorite retail outlet.*

## HARLEQUIN®
*Makes any time special* ™

**Look for a new and exciting series from Harlequin!**

# HARLEQUIN Duets™

*Two __new__ full-length novels in one book, from some of your favorite authors!*

Starting in May, each month we'll be bringing you two new books, each book containing two brand-new stories about the lighter side of love! Double the pleasure, double the romance, for less than the cost of two regular romance titles!

Look for these two new Harlequin Duets™ titles in May 1999:

Book 1:
WITH A STETSON AND A SMILE
by Vicki Lewis Thompson
THE BRIDESMAID'S BET
by Christie Ridgway

Book 2:
KIDNAPPED? by Jacqueline Diamond
I GOT YOU, BABE by Bonnie Tucker

**2 GREAT STORIES BY 2 GREAT AUTHORS FOR 1 LOW PRICE!**

*Don't miss it! Available May 1999 at your favorite retail outlet.*

HARLEQUIN®
*Makes any time special.*™

Look us up on-line at: http://www.romance.net          HDGENR

# HARLEQUIN®
*Makes any time special* ™

WIN A DREAM

# In celebration of Harlequin®'s golden anniversary

Enter to win a *dream!* You could win:

- A luxurious trip for two to **The Renaissance Cottonwoods Resort** in Scottsdale, Arizona, or

- A bouquet of flowers once a week for a year from **FTD**, or

- A $500 shopping spree, or

- A fabulous bath & body gift basket, including **K-tel's** *Candlelight and Romance* 5-CD set.

Look for **WIN A DREAM** flash on specially marked Harlequin® titles by Penny Jordan, Dallas Schulze, Anne Stuart and Kristine Rolofson in October 1999*.

## RENAISSANCE. COTTONWOODS RESORT
SCOTTSDALE, ARIZONA

K·TEL

*No purchase necessary—for contest details send a self-addressed envelope to Harlequin Makes Any Time Special Contest, P.O. Box 9069, Buffalo, NY, 14269-9069 (include contest name on self-addressed envelope). Contest ends December 31, 1999. Open to U.S. and Canadian residents who are 18 or over. Void where prohibited.

PHMATS-GR

# COMING NEXT MONTH

### #745 BABY.COM Molly Liholm
**Bachelors & Babies**

When bachelor Sam Evans finds a baby on his doorstep he's surprised. Little Juliette even comes with a web page and care instructions! *Then* Anne Logan appears on Sam's doorstep. The sexy nanny agrees to help, but soon she doesn't know *who* is more trouble—the teething tot or lovesick Sam!

### #746 A CLASS ACT Pamela Burford
**15th Anniversary Celebration!**

Voted "Most Likely To...Succeed," lawyer Gabe Moreau has done exactly that. But he's never forgotten gorgeous Dena Devlin. Time hasn't erased the hurt...or the hot sizzling attraction between them. Their high school reunion will be the perfect place to reignite those feelings....

### #747 NIGHT WHISPERS Leslie Kelly

DJ Kelsey Logan knows what she wants—stuffy but sexy Mitch Wymore. So what if the handsome prof doesn't care for her late-night radio venue "Night Whispers"! It's a show about romance and fantasy—two things Kelsey is absolutely convinced Mitch needs in his life....

### #748 THE SEDUCTION OF SYDNEY Jamie Denton
**Blaze**

Sydney Travers's biological clock is ticking loudly, but there's no suitable daddy in sight. Except Derek Buchanan, who is her best friend and *hardly* lover material. But Sydney has no idea the sexy scientist is in love with her—and determined to seduce Sydney at the first opportunity.